OUT

OF THE

STORM

UNCOLLECTED
FANTASIES BY

**WILLIAM
HOPE
HODGSON**

EDITED BY SAM MOSKOWITZ

ILLUSTRATED BY STEPHEN FABIAN

CENTAUR BOOKS, INC.
NEW YORK
1980

OUT OF THE STORM
by William Hope Hodgson

Copyright © 1975 by Sam Moskowitz

Printed in the United States of America

ISBN 0-87818-016-8

Centaur Books edition — first published 1980

Distributed by
Como Sales, Inc.
799 Broadway, New York, N.Y. 10003

CONTENTS

Page

ILLUSTRATIONS

A Tropical Horror

A TROPICAL HORROR

We are a hundred and thirty days out from Melbourne, and for three weeks we have lain in this sweltering calm.

It is midnight, and our watch on deck until four a.m. I go out and sit on the hatch. A minute later, Joky, our youngest 'prentice, joins me for a chatter. Many are the hours we have sat thus and talked in the night watches; though, to be sure, it is Joky who does the talking. I am content to smoke and listen, giving an occasional grunt at seasons to show that I am attentive.

Joky has been silent for some time, his head bent in meditation. Suddenly he looks up, evidently with the intention of making some remark. As he does so, I see his face stiffen with a nameless horror. He crouches back, his eyes staring past me at some unseen fear. Then his mouth opens. He gives forth a strangulated cry and topples backward off the hatch, striking his head against the deck. Fearing I know not what, I turn to look.

7

Great Heavens! Rising above the bulwarks, seen plainly in the bright moonlight, is a vast slobbering mouth a fathom across. From the huge dripping lips hang great tentacles. As I look the Thing comes further over the rail. It is rising, rising, higher and higher. There are no eyes visible; only that fearful slobbering mouth set on the tremendous trunk-like neck; which, even as I watch, is curling inboard with the stealthy celerity of an enormous eel. Over it comes in vast heaving folds. Will it never end? The ship gives a slow, sullen roll to starboard as she feels the weight. Then the tail, a broad, flat-shaped mass, slips over the teak rail and falls with a loud slump on to the deck.

For a few seconds the hideous creature lies heaped in writhing, slimy coils. Then, with quick, darting movements, the monstrous head travels along the deck. Close by the mainmast stand the harness casks, and alongside of these a freshly opened cask of salt beef with the top loosely replaced. The smell of the meat seems to attract the monster, and I can hear it sniffing with a vast indrawing breath. Then those lips open, displaying four huge fangs; there is a quick forward motion of the head, a sudden crashing, crunching sound, and beef and barrel have disappeared. The noise brings one of the ordinary seamen out of the fo'cas'le. Coming into the night, he can see nothing for a moment. Then, as he gets further aft, he *sees,* and with horrified cries rushes forward. Too late! From the mouth of the Thing there flashes forth a long, broad blade of glistening white, set with fierce teeth. I avert my eyes, but cannot shut out the sickening "Glut! Glut!" that follows.

The man on the "look-out," attracted by the disturbance, has witnessed the tragedy, and flies for refuge into the fo'cas'le, flinging to the heavy iron door after him.

The carpenter and sailmaker come running out from the half-deck in their drawers. Seeing the awful Thing, they rush aft to the cabin with shouts of fear. The second mate, after one glance over the break of the poop, runs down the companion-way with the helmsman after him. I can hear them barring the scuttle, and abruptly I realise that I am on the main deck alone.

So far I have forgotten my own danger. The past few minutes seem like a portion of an awful dream. Now, however, I comprehend my position and, shaking off the horror that has held me, turn to seek safety. As I do so my eyes fall upon Joky, lying huddled and senseless with fright where he has fallen. I cannot leave him there. Close by stands the empty half-deck — a little steel-built house with iron doors. The lee one is hooked open. Once inside I am safe.

Up to the present the Thing has seemed to be unconscious of my presence. Now, however, the huge barrel-like head sways in my direction; then comes a muffled bellow, and the great tongue flickers in and out as the brute turns and swirls aft to meet me. I know there is not a moment to lose, and, picking up the helpless lad, I make a run for the open door. It is only distant a few yards, but that awful shape is coming down the deck to me in great wreathing coils. I reach the house and tumble in with my burden; then out on deck again to unhook and close the door. Even as I do so something white curls round the end of the house. With a bound I am inside and the door is shut and bolted. Through the thick glass of the ports I see the Thing sweep round the house, in vain search for me.

Joky has not moved yet; so, kneeling down, I loosen his shirt collar and sprinkle some water from the breaker over his face. While I am doing this I hear Morgan shout something; then comes a great shriek of terror, and again that sickening "Glut! Glut!"

Joky stirs uneasily, rubs his eyes, and sits up suddenly.

"Was that Morgan shouting — ?" He breaks off with a cry. "Where are we? I have had such awful dreams!"

At this instant there is a sound of running footsteps on the deck and I hear Morgan's voice at the door.

"Tom, open — !"

He stops abruptly and gives an awful cry of despair. Then I hear him rush forward. Through the porthole, I see him spring into the fore rigging and scramble madly aloft. Something steals up after him. It shows white in the moonlight. It wraps itself around his right ankle. Morgan stops dead, plucks out his sheath-knife, and hacks fiercely at the fiend-ish thing. It lets go, and in a second he is over the top and running for dear life up the t'gallant rigging.

A time of quietness follows, and presently I see that the day is breaking. Not a sound can be heard save the heavy gasping breathing of the Thing. As the sun rises higher the creature stretches itself out along the deck and seems to enjoy the warmth. Still no sound, either from the men forward or the officers aft. I can only suppose that they are afraid of attract-ing its attention. Yet, a little later, I hear the report of a pistol away aft, and looking out I see the serpent raise its huge head as though listening. As it does so I get a good view of the fore part, and in the daylight see what the night has hidden.

There, right about the mouth, is a pair of little pig-eyes, that seem to twinkle with a diabolical intelligence. It is swaying its head slowly from side to side; then, without warning, it turns quickly and looks right in through the port. I dodge out of sight; but not soon enough. It has seen me, and brings its great mouth up against the glass.

I hold my breath. My God! If it breaks the glass! I cower, horrified. From the direction of the port there comes a loud, harsh, scraping sound. I shiver. Then I remember that there are little iron doors to shut over the ports in bad weather. Without a moment's waste of time I rise to my feet and slam to the door over the port. Then I go round to the others and do the same. We are now in darkness, and I tell Joky in a whisper to light the lamp, which, after some fumbling, he does.

About an hour before midnight I fall asleep. I am awakened suddenly some hours later by a scream of agony and the rattle of a water-dipper. There is a slight scuffling sound; then that soul-revolting "Glut! Glut!"

I guess what has happened. One of the men forrad has slipped out of the fo'cas'le to try and get a little water. Evidently he has trusted to the darkness to hide his movements. Poor beggar! He has paid for his attempt with his life!

After this I cannot sleep, though the rest of the night passes quietly enough. Towards morning I doze a bit, but wake every few minutes with a start. Joky is sleeping peacefully; indeed, he seems worn out with the terrible strain of the past twenty-four hours. About eight a.m. I call him, and we make a light breakfast off the dry ship's biscuit and water. Of the latter happily we have a good supply. Joky seems more himself, and starts to talk a little — possibly somewhat louder than is safe; for, as he chatters on, wondering how it will end, there comes a tremendous blow against the side of the house, making it ring again. After this Joky is very silent. As we sit there I cannot but wonder what all the rest are doing, and how the poor beggars forrad are faring, cooped up without water, as the tragedy of the night has proved.

Towards noon, I hear a loud bang, followed by a terrific bellowing. Then comes a great smashing of woodwork, and the cries of men in pain. Vainly I ask myself what has happened. I begin to reason. By the sound of the report it was evidently something much heavier than a rifle or pistol, and judging from the mad roaring of the Thing, the shot must have done some execution. On thinking it over further, I become convinced that, by some means, those aft have got hold of the small signal cannon we carry, and though I know that some have been hurt, perhaps killed, yet a feeling of exultation seizes me as I listen to the roars of the Thing, and realise that it is badly wounded, perhaps mortally. After a while, however, the bellowing dies away, and only an occasional roar, denoting more of anger than aught else, is heard.

Presently I become aware, by the ship's canting over to starboard, that the creature has gone over to that side, and a great hope springs up within me that possibly it has had enough of us and is going over the rail into the sea. For a time all is silent and my hope grows stronger. I lean across and nudge Joky, who is sleeping with his head on the table. He starts up sharply with a loud cry.

"Hush!" I whisper hoarsely. "I'm not certain, but I do believe it's gone."

Joky's face brightens wonderfully, and he questions me eagerly. We wait another hour or so, with hope ever rising. Our confidence is returning fast. Not a sound can we hear, not even the breathing of the Beast. I get out some biscuits, and Joky, after rummaging in the locker, produces a small piece of pork and a bottle of ship's vinegar. We fall to with a relish. After our long abstinence from food the meal acts on us like wine, and what must Joky do but insist on opening the door, to make sure the Thing has gone. This I will not allow, telling him that at least it will be safer to open the iron port-covers first and have a look out. Joky argues, but I am immovable. He becomes excited. I believe the youngster is light-headed. Then, as I turn to unscrew one of the after-covers, Joky makes a dash at the door. Before he can undo the bolts I have him, and after a short struggle lead him back to the table. Even as I endeavour to quieten him there comes at the starboard door — the door that Joky has tried to open — a sharp, loud sniff, sniff, followed immediately by a thunderous grunting howl and a foul stench of putrid breath sweeps in under the door. A great trembling takes me, and were it not for the carpenter's tool-chest I should fall. Joky turns very white and is violently sick, after which he is seized by a hopeless fit of sobbing.

Hour after hour passes, and, weary to death, I lie

down on the chest upon which I have been sitting, and try to rest.

It must be about half-past two in the morning, after a somewhat longer doze, that I am suddenly awakened by a most tremendous uproar away forrad — men's voices shrieking, cursing, praying; but in spite of the terror expressed, so weak and feeble; while in the midst, and at times broken off short with that hellishly suggestive "Glut! Glut!" is the unearthly bellowing of the Thing. Fear incarnate seizes me, and I can only fall on my knees and pray. Too well I know what is happening.

Joky has slept through it all, and I am thankful.

Presently, under the door there steals a narrow ribbon of light, and I know that the day has broken on the second morning of our imprisonment. I let Joky sleep on. I will let him have peace while he may. Time passes, but I take little notice. The Thing is quiet, probably sleeping. About midday I eat a little biscuit and drink some of the water. Joky still sleeps. It is best so.

A sound breaks the stillness. The ship gives a slight heave, and I know that once more the Thing is awake. Round the deck it moves, causing the ship to roll perceptibly. Once it goes forrad — I fancy to again explore the fo'cas'le. Evidently it finds nothing, for it returns almost immediately. It pauses a moment at the house, then goes on further aft. Up aloft, somewhere in the fore-rigging, there rings out a peal of wild laughter, though sounding very faint and far away. The Horror stops suddenly. I listen intently, but hear nothing save a sharp creaking beyond the after end of the house, as though a strain had come upon the rigging.

A minute later I hear a cry aloft, followed almost instantly by a loud crash on deck that seems to shake the ship. I wait in anxious fear. What is happening? The minutes pass slowly. Then comes another frightened shout. It ceases suddenly. The suspense has become terrible, and I am no longer able to bear it. Very cautiously I open one of the after port-covers, and peep out to see a fearful sight. There, with its tail upon the deck and its vast body curled round the mainmast, is the monster, its head above the topsail yard, and its great claw-armed tentacle waving in the air. It is the first proper sight that I have had of the Thing. Good Heavens! It must weigh a hundred tons! Knowing that I shall have time, I open the port itself, then crane my head out and look up. There on the extreme end of the lower topsail yard I see one of the able seamen. Even down here I note the staring horror of his face. At this moment he sees me and gives a weak, hoarse cry for help. I can do nothing for him. As I look the great tongue shoots out and licks him off the yard, much as might a dog a fly off the window-pane.

Higher still, but happily out of reach, are two more of the men. As far as I can judge they are lashed to the mast above the royal yard. The Thing attempts to reach them, but after a futile effort it ceases, and starts to slide down, coil on coil, to the deck. While doing this I notice a great gaping wound on its body some twenty feet above the tail.

I drop my gaze from aloft and look aft. The cabin door is torn from its hinges, and the bulkhead — which, unlike the half-deck, is of teak wood — is partly broken down. With a shudder I realise the cause of those cries after the cannon-shot. Turning I screw my head round and try to see the foremast, but cannot. The sun, I notice, is low, and the night is near. Then I draw in my head and fasten up both port and cover.

How will it end? Oh! how will it end?

After a while Joky wakes up. He is very restless, yet though he has eaten nothing during the day I cannot get him to touch anything.

Night draws on. We are too weary — too dispirited to talk. I lie down, but not to sleep. . . . Time passes.

* * * * *

A ventilator rattles violently somewhere on the main deck, and there sounds constantly that slurring, gritty noise. Later I hear a cat's agonised howl, and then again all is quiet. Some time after comes a great splash alongside. Then, for some hours all is silent as the grave. Occasionally I sit up on the chest and listen, yet never a whisper of noise comes to me. There is an absolute silence, even the monotonous creak of the gear has died away entirely, and at last a real hope is springing up within me. That splash, this silence — surely I am justified in hoping. I do not wake Joky this time. I will prove first for myself that all is safe. Still I wait. I will run no unnecessary risks. After a time I creep to the after-port and will listen; but there is no sound. I put up my hand and feel at the screw, then again I hesitate, yet not for long. Noiselessly I begin to unscrew the fastening of the heavy shield. It swings loose on its hinge, and I pull it back and peer out. My heart is beating madly. Everything seems strangely dark outside. Perhaps the moon has gone behind a cloud. Suddenly a beam of moonlight enters through the port, and goes as quickly. I stare out. Something moves. Again the light streams in, and now I seem to be looking into a great cavern, at the bottom of which quivers and curls something palely white.

My heart seems to stand still! It is the Horror! I start back and seize the iron port-flap to slam it to. As I do so, something strikes the glass like a steam ram, shatters it to atoms, and flicks past me into the berth. I scream and spring away. The port is quite filled with it. The lamp shows it dimly. It is curling and twisting here and there. It is as thick as a tree, and covered with a smooth slimy skin. At the end is a

great claw, like a lobster's, only a thousand times larger. I cower down into the farthest corner. . . . It has broken the tool-chest to pieces with one click of those frightful mandibles. Joky has crawled under a bunk. The Thing sweeps round in my direction. I feel a drop of sweat trickle slowly down my face — it tastes salty. Nearer comes that awful death. . . . Crash! I roll over backwards. It has crushed the water breaker against which I leant, and I am rolling in the water across the floor. The claw drives up, then down, with a quick uncertain movement, striking the deck a dull, heavy blow, a foot from my head. Joky gives a little gasp of horror. Slowly the Thing rises and starts feeling its way round the berth. It plunges into a bunk and pulls out a bolster, nips it in half and drops it, then moves on. It is feeling along the deck. As it does so it comes across a half of the bolster. It seems to toy with it, then picks it up and takes it out through the port. . . .

A wave of putrid air fills the berth. There is a grating sound, and something enters the port again — something white and tapering and set with teeth. Hither and thither it curls, rasping over the bunks, ceiling, and deck, with a noise like that of a great saw at work. Twice it flickers above my head, and I close my eyes. Then off it goes again. It sounds now on the opposite side of the berth and nearer to Joky. Suddenly the harsh, raspy noise becomes muffled, as though the teeth were passing across some soft substance. Joky gives a horrid little scream, that breaks off into a bubbling, whistling sound. I open my eyes. The tip of the vast tongue is curled tightly round something that drips, then is quickly withdrawn, allowing the moonbeams to steal again into the berth. I rise to my feet. Looking round, I note in a mechanical sort of way the wrecked state of the berth — the shattered chests, dismantled bunks, and something else —

"Joky!" I cry, and tingle all over.

There is that awful Thing again at the port. I glance round for a weapon. I will revenge Joky. Ah! there, right under the lamp, where the wreck of the carpenter's chest strews the floor, lies a small hatchet. I spring forward and seize it. It is small, but so keen — so keen! I feel its razor edge lovingly. Then I am back at the port. I stand to one side and raise my weapon. The great tongue is feeling its way to those fearsome remains. It reaches them. As it does so, with a scream of "Joky! Joky!" I strike savagely again and again and again, gasping as I strike; once more, and the monstrous mass falls to the deck, writhing like a hideous eel. A vast, warm flood rushes in through the porthole. There is a sound of breaking steel and an enormous bellowing. A singing comes in my ears and grows louder — louder. Then the berth grows indistinct and suddenly dark.

* * * * *

Extract from the log of the steamship *Hispaniola.*
June 24. — Lat. — N. Long. — W. 11 a.m. —
Sighted four-masted barque about four points on the
port bow, flying signal of distress. Ran down to her
and sent a boat aboard. She proved to be the *Glen
Doon,* homeward bound from Melbourne to London.
Found things in a terrible state. Decks covered with
blood and slime. Steel deck-house stove in. Broke
open door, and discovered youth of about nineteen
in last stage of inanition, also part remains of boy
about fourteen years of age. There was a great quantity of blood in the place, and a huge curled-up mass
of whitish flesh, weighing about half a ton, one end of
which appeared to have been hacked through with a
sharp instrument. Found forecastle door open and
hanging from one hinge. Doorway bulged, as though
something had been forced through. Went inside.
Terrible state of affairs, blood everywhere, broken
chests, smashed bunks, but no men nor remains.
Went aft again and found youth showing signs of
recovery. When he came round, gave the name of
Thompson. Said they had been attacked by a huge
serpent — thought it must have been sea-serpent. He
was too weak to say much, but told us there were
some men up the mainmast. Sent a hand aloft, who
reported them lashed to the royal mast, and quite
dead. Went aft to the cabin. Here we found the bulkhead smashed to pieces, and the cabin-door lying on
the deck near the after-hatch. Found body of captain

down lazarette, but no officers. Noticed amongst the wreckage part of the carriage of a small cannon. Came aboard again.

Have sent the second mate with six men to work her into port. Thompson is with us. He has written out his version of the affair. We certainly consider that the state of the ship, as we found her, bears out in every respect his story. (Signed)

William Norton (Master).
Tom Briggs (1st Mate).

Out of the Storm

OUT OF THE STORM

"Hush!" said my friend the scientist, as I walked into his laboratory. I had opened my lips to speak; but stood silent for a few minutes at his request.

He was sitting at his instrument, and the thing was tapping out a message in a curiously irregular fashion — stopping a few seconds, then going on at a furious pace.

It was during a somewhat longer than usual pause that, growing slightly impatient, I ventured to address him.

"Anything important?" I asked.

"For God's sake, shut up!" he answered back in a high, strained voice.

I stared. I am used to pretty abrupt treatment from him at times when he is much engrossed in some particular experiment; but this was going a little too far, and I said so.

He was writing, and, for reply, he pushed several loosely-written sheets over to me with the one curt word, "Read!".

With a sense half of anger, half of curiosity, I

27

picked up the first and glanced at it. After a few lines, I was gripped and held securely by a morbid interest. I was reading a message from one in the last extremity. I will give it word for word: —

"John, we are sinking! I wonder if you really understand what I feel at the present time — you sitting comfortably in your laboratory, I out here upon the waters, already one among the dead. Yes, we are doomed. There is no such thing as help in our case. We are sinking — steadily, remorselessly. God! I must keep up and be a man! I need not tell you that I am in the operator's room. All the rest are on deck — or dead in the hungry thing which is smashing the ship to pieces.

"I do not know where we are, and there is no one of whom I can ask. The last of the officers was drowned nearly an hour ago, and the vessel is now little more than a sort of breakwater for the giant seas.

"Once, about half an hour ago, I went out on to the deck. My God! the sight was terrible. It is a little after midday; but the sky is the color of mud — do you understand? — gray mud! Down from it there hang vast lappets of clouds. Not such clouds as I have ever before seen; but monstrous, mildewed-looking hulls. They show solid, save where the frightful wind tears their lower edges into great feelers that swirl savagely above us, like the tentacles of some enormous Horror.

"Such a sight is difficult to describe to the living; though the Dead of the Sea know of it without words of mine. It is such a sight that none is allowed to see and live. It is a picture for the doomed and the dead; one of the sea's hell-orgies — one of the *Thing's* monstrous gloatings over the living —say the alive-in-death, those upon the brink. I have no right to tell of it to you; to speak of it to one of the living is to initiate innocence into one of the infernal mysteries — to talk of foul things to a child. Yet I care not! I will expose, in all its hideous nakedness, the death-side of the sea. The undoomed living shall know some of the things that death has hitherto so well guarded. Death knows not of this little instrument beneath my hands that connects me still with the quick, else would he haste to quiet me.

"Hark you, John! I have learnt undreamt of things in this little time of waiting. I know now why we are afraid of the dark. I had never imagined such secrets of the sea and the grave (which are one and the same).

"Listen! Ah, but I was forgetting you cannot hear! I can! The Sea is — Hush! the Sea is laughing, as though Hell cackled from the mouth of an ass. It is jeering. I can hear its voice echo like Satanic thunder amid the mud overhead — It is calling to me! call— I must go — The sea calls!

"Oh! God, art Thou indeed God? Canst Thou sit

above and watch calmly that which I have just seen?
Nay! Thou art no God! Thou art weak and puny
beside this foul *Thing* which Thou didst create in Thy
lusty youth. *It* is *now* God — and I am one of its
children.

"Are you there, John? Why don't you answer!
Listen! I ignore God; for there is a stronger than He.
My God is here, beside me, around me, and will be
soon above me. You know what that means. It is
merciless. *The sea is now all the God there is!* That is one
of the things I have learnt.

"Listen! *it,* is laughing again. God is *it,* not He.

"It called, and I went out on to the decks. All
was terrible. *It* is in the waist — everywhere. *It* has
swamped the ship. Only the forecastle, bridge and
poop stick up out from the bestial, reeking *Thing*, like
three islands in the midst of shrieking foam. At times
gigantic billows assail the ship from both sides. They
form momentary arches above the vessel — arches of
dull, curved water half a hundred feet towards the
hideous sky. Then they descend —roaring. Think of
it! You cannot.

"There is an infection of sin in the air: it is the
exhalations from the *Thing*. Those left upon the
drenched islets of shattered wood and iron are doing
the most horrible things. The *Thing* is teaching them.
Later, I felt the vile informing of its breath; but I
have fled back here — to pray for death.

"On the forecastle, I saw a mother and her little

son clinging to an iron rail. A great billow heaved up above them — descended in a falling mountain of brine. It passed, and they were still there. The *Thing* was only toying with them; yet, all the same, it had torn the hands of the child from the rail, and the child was clinging frantically to its Mother's arm. I saw another vast hill hurl up to port and hover above them. Then the Mother stooped and bit like a foul beast at the hands of her wee son. She was afraid that his little additional weight would be more than she could hold. I heard his scream even where I stood — it drove to me upon that wild laughter. It told me again that God is not He, but *It.* Then the hill thundered down upon those two. It seemed to me that the *Thing* gave a bellow as it leapt. It roared about them churning and growling; then surged away, and there was only one — the Mother. There appeared to me to be blood as well as water upon her face, especially about her mouth; but the distance was too great, and I cannot be sure. I looked away. Close to me, I saw something further — a beautiful young girl (her soul hideous with the breath of the *Thing*) struggling with her sweetheart for the shelter of the charthouse side. He threw her off; but she came back at him. I saw her hand come from her head, where still clung the wreckage of some form of headgear. She struck at him. He shouted and fell away to leeward, and she — smiled, showing her teeth. So much for that. I turned elsewhere.

"Out upon the *Thing,* I saw gleams, horrid and

suggestive, below the crests of the waves. I have never seen them until this time. I saw a rough sailorman washed away from the vessel. One of the huge breakers snapped at him! — Those things were teeth. *It* has teeth. I heard them clash. I heard his yell. It was no more than a mosquito's shrilling amid all that laughter; but it was very terrible. There is worse than death.

"The ship is lurching very queerly with a sort of sickening heave —

"I fancy I have been asleep. No — I remember now. I hit my head when she rolled so strangely. My leg is doubled under me. I think it is broken; but it does not matter —

"I have been praying. I — I — What was it? I feel calmer, more resigned, now. I think I have been mad. What was it that I was saying? I cannot remember. It was something about — about — God. I — I believe I blasphemed. May He forgive me! Thou knowest, God, that I was not in my right mind. Thou knowest that I am very weak. Be with me in the coming time! I have sinned; but Thou art all merciful.

"Are you there, John? It is very near the end now. I had so much to say; but it all slips from me. What was it that I said? I take it all back. I was mad, and — and God knows. He is merciful, and I have very little pain now. I feel a bit drowsy.

"I wonder whether you are there, John. Perhaps, after all, no one has heard the things I have said. It is better so. The Living are not meant — and yet, I do not know. If you are there, John, you will — you will tell *her* how it was; but not — not — Hark! there was such a thunder of water overhead just then. I fancy two vast seas have met in mid-air across the top of the bridge and burst all over the vessel. It must be soon now — and there was such a number of things I had to say! I can hear voices in the wind. They are singing. It is like an enormous dirge —

"I think I have been dozing again. I pray God humbly that it be soon! You will not — not tell *her* anything about, about what I may have said, will you, John? I mean those things which I ought not to have said. What was it I did say? My head is growing strangely confused. I wonder whether you really do hear me. I may be talking only to that vast roar outside. Still, it is some comfort to go on, and I will not believe that you do not hear all I say. Hark again! A mountain of brine must have swept clean over the vessel. She has gone right over on to her side. . . . She is back again. It will be very soon now —

"Are you there, John? Are you there? It is coming! The Sea has come for me! It is rushing down through the companionway! It — it is like a vast jet! My God! I am dr-own-ing! I — am — dr —"

The Finding of the Graiken

THE FINDING OF THE GRAIKEN

When a year had passed, and still there was no news of the full-rigged ship Graiken, even the most sanguine of my old chum's friends had ceased to hope perchance, somewhere, she might be above water.

Yet Ned Barlow, in his inmost thoughts, I knew, still hugged to himself the hope that she would win home. Poor, dear old fellow, how my heart did go out towards him in his sorrow!

For it was in the Graiken that his sweetheart had sailed on that dull January day some twelve months previously.

The voyage had been taken for the sake of her health; yet since then — save for a distant signal recorded at the Azores — there had been from all the mystery of ocean no voice; the ship and they within her had vanished utterly.

And still Barlow hoped. He said nothing actually, but at times his deeper thoughts would float up and show through the sea of his usual talk, and thus I would know in an indirect way of the thing that his heart was thinking.

Nor was time a healer.

It was later that my present good fortune came to me. My uncle died, and I — hitherto poor — was now a rich man. In a breath, it seemed, I had become possessor of houses, lands, and money; also — in my eyes almost more important — a fine fore-and-aft-rigged yacht of some two hundred tons register.

It seemed scarcely believable that the thing was mine, and I was all in a scutter to run away down to Falmouth and get to sea.

In old times, when my uncle had been more than usually gracious, he had invited me to accompany him for a trip round the coast or elsewhere, as the fit might take him; yet never, even in my most hopeful moments, had it occurred to me that ever she might be mine.

And now I was hurrying my preparations for a good long sea trip — for to me the sea is, and always has been, a comrade.

Still, with all the prospects before me, I was by no means completely satisfied, for I wanted Ned Barlow with me, and yet was afraid to ask him.

I had the feeling that, in view of his overwhelming loss, he must positively hate the sea; and yet I could not be happy at the thought of leaving him, and going alone.

He had not been well lately, and a sea voyage would be the very thing for him, if only it were not going to freshen painful memories.

Eventually I decided to suggest it, and this I did a couple of days before the date I had fixed for sailing.

"Ned," I said, "you need a change."

"Yes," he assented wearily.

"Come with me, old chap," I went on, growing bolder. "I'm taking a trip in the yacht. It would be splendid to have —"

To my dismay, he jumped to his feet and came towards me excitedly.

"I've upset him now," was my thought. "I *am* a fool!"

"Go to sea!" he said. "My God! I'd give — " He broke off short, and stood suppressed opposite to me, his face all of a quiver with suppressed emotion. He was silent a few seconds, getting himself in hand; then he proceeded more quietly: "Where to!"

"Anywhere," I replied, watching him keenly, for I was greatly puzzled by his manner. "I'm not quite clear yet. Somewhere south of here — the West Indies, I have thought. It's all so new, you know —just fancy being able to go just where we like. I can hardly realise it yet."

I stopped, for he had turned from me and was staring out of the window.

"You'll come, Ned?" I cried, fearful that he was going to refuse me.

He took a pace away, and came back.

"I'll come," he said, and there was a look of

strange excitement in his eyes that set me off on a tack of vague wonder; but I said nothing, just told him how he had pleased me.

II.

We had been at sea a couple of weeks, and were alone upon the Atlantic — at least, so much of it as presented itself to our view.

I was leaning over the taffrail, staring down into the boil of the wake; yet I noticed nothing, for I was wrapped in a tissue of somewhat uncomfortable thought. It was about Ned Barlow.

He had been queer, decidedly queer, since leaving port. His whole attitude mentally had been that of a man under the influence of an all-pervading excitement. I had said that he was in need of change, and had trusted that the splendid tonic of the sea breeze would serve to put him soon to rights mentally and physically; yet here was the poor old chap acting in a manner calculated to cause me anxiety as to his balance.

Scarcely a word had been spoken since leaving the Channel. When I ventured to speak to him, often he would take not the least notice, other times he would answer only by a brief word; but talk — never.

In addition, his whole time was spent on deck among the men, and with some of them he seemed to converse both long and earnestly; yet to me, his chum and true friend, not a word.

Another thing came to me as a surprise —Barlow betrayed the greatest interest in the position of the vessel, and the courses set, all in such a manner as left me no room for doubt but that his knowledge of navigation was considerable.

Once I ventured to express my astonishment at this knowledge, and ask a question or two as to the way in which he had gathered it, but had been treated with such an absurdly stony silence that since then I had not spoken to him.

With all this it may be easily conceived that my thoughts, as I stared down into the wake, were troublesome.

Suddenly I heard a voice at my elbow:

"I should like to have a word with you, sir." I turned sharply. It was my skipper, and something in his face told me that all was not as it should be.

"Well, Jenkins, fire away."

He looked round, as if afraid of being overheard; then came closer to me.

"Someone's been messing with the compasses, sir," he said in a low voice.

"What?" I asked sharply.

"They've been meddled with, sir. The magnets have been shifted, and by someone who's a good idea of what he's doing."

"What on earth do you mean?" I inquired.

"Why should anyone mess about with them? What good would it do them? You must be mistaken."

"No, sir, I'm not. They've been touched within the last forty-eight hours, and by someone that understands what he's doing."

I stared at him. The man was so certain. I felt bewildered.

"But why should they?"

"That's more than I can say, sir; but it's a serious matter, and I want to know what I'm to do. It looks to me as though there were something funny going on. I'd give a month's pay to know just who it was, for certain."

"Well," I said, "if they have been touched, it can only be by one of the officers. You say the chap who has done it must understand what he is doing."

He shook his head. "No, sir — " he began, and then stopped abruptly. His gaze met mine. I think the same thought must have come to us simultaneously. I gave a little gasp of amazement.

He wagged his head at me. "I've had my suspicions for a bit, sir," he went on; "but seeing that he's —he's — " He was fairly struck for the moment.

I took my weight off the rail and stood upright.

"To whom are you referring?" I asked curtly.

"Why, sir, to him — Mr. Ned — "

He would have gone on, but I cut him short.

"That will do, Jenkins!" I cried. "Mr. Ned Barlow is my friend. You are forgetting yourself a

little. You will accuse me of tampering with the compasses next!"

I turned away, leaving little Captain Jenkins
speechless. I had spoken with an almost vehement
over-loyalty, to quiet my own suspicions.

All the same, I was horribly bewildered, not
knowing what to think or do or say, so that,
eventually, I did just nothing.

III.

It was early one morning, about a week later,
that I opened my eyes abruptly. I was lying on my
back in my bunk, and the daylight was beginning to
creep wanly in through the ports.

I had a vague consciousness that all was not as it
should be, and feeling thus, I made to grasp the edge
of my bunk, and sit up, but failed, owing to the fact
that my wrists were securely fastened by a pair of
heavy steel handcuffs.

Utterly confounded, I let my head fall back
upon the pillow; and then, in the midst of my
bewilderment, there sounded the sharp report of a
pistol-shot somewhere on the decks over my head.
There came a second, and the sound of voices and
footsteps, and then a long spell of silence.

Into my mind had rushed the single word —
mutiny! My temples throbbed a little, but I strug-

gled to keep calm and think, and then, all adrift, I fell to searching round for a reason. Who was it? And why?

Perhaps an hour passed, during which I asked myself ten thousand vain questions. All at once I heard a key inserted in the door. So I had been locked in! It turned, and the steward walked into the cabin. He did not look at me, but went to the arm-rack and began to remove the various weapons.

"What the devil is the meaning of all this, Jones?" I roared, getting up a bit on one elbow. "What's happened?"

But the fool answered not a word — just went to and fro carrying out the weapons from my cabin into the next, so that at last I ceased from questioning him, and lay silent, promising myself future vengeance.

When he had removed the arms, the steward began to go through my table drawers, emptying them, so that it appeared to me, of everything that could be used as a weapon or tool.

Having completed his task, he vanished, locking the door after him.

Some time passed, and at last, about seven bells, he reappeared, this time bringing a tray with my breakfast. Placing it upon the table, he came across to me and proceeded to unlock the cuffs from off my wrists. Then for the first time he spoke.

"Mr. Barlow desires me to say, sir, that you are

to have the liberty of your cabin so long as you will agree not to cause any bother. Should you wish for anything, I am under his orders to supply you." He retreated hastily toward the door.

On my part, I was almost speechless with astonishment and rage.

"One minute, Jones!" I shouted, just as he was in the act of leaving the cabin. "Kindly explain what you mean. You said Mr. Barlow. Is it to him that I owe all this?" And I waved my hand towards the irons which the man still held.

"It is by his orders," replied he, and turned once more to leave the cabin.

"I don't understand!" I said, bewildered. "Mr. Barlow is my friend, and this is my yacht! By what right do you dare to take your orders from him? Let me out!"

As I shouted the last command, I leapt from my bunk, and made a dash for the door, but the steward, so far from attempting to bar it, flung it open and stepped quickly through, thus allowing me to see that a couple of the sailors were stationed in the alleyway.

"Get on deck at once!" I said angrily. "What are you doing down here?"

"Sorry sir," said one of the men. "We'd take it kindly if you'd make no trouble. But we ain't lettin' you out, sir. Don't make no bloomin' error."

I hesitated, then went to the table and sat down.

I would, at least, do my best to preserve my dignity.

After an inquiry as to whether he could do anything further, the steward left me to breakfast and my thoughts. As may be imagined, the latter were by no means pleasant.

Here was I prisoner in my own yacht, and by the hand of the very man I had loved and befriended through many years. Oh, it was too incredible and mad!

For a while, leaving the table, I paced the deck of my room; then, growing calmer, I sat down again and attempted to make some sort of a meal.

As I breakfasted, my chief thought was as to *why* my one-time chum was treating me thus; and after that I fell to puzzling *how* he had managed to get the yacht into his own hands.

Many things came back to me — his familiarity with the men, his treatment of me — which I had put down to a temporary want of balance — the fooling with the compasses; for I was certain now that he had been the doer of that piece of mischief. But *why?* That was the great point.

As I turned the matter over in my brain, an incident that had occurred some six days back came to me. It had been on the very day after the captain's report to me of the tampering with the compasses.

Barlow had, for the first time, relinquished his brooding and silence, and had started to talk to me, but in such a wild strain that he had made me feel vaguely uncomfortable about his sanity for he told me some wild yarn of an idea which he had got into his head. And then, in an overbearing way, he demanded that the navigating of the yacht should be put into his hands.

He had been very incoherent, and was plainly in a state of considerable mental excitement. He had rambled on about some derelict, and then had talked in an extraordinary fashion of a vast world of seaweed.

Once or twice in his bewilderingly disconnected speech he had mentioned the name of his sweetheart, and now it was the memory of her name that gave me the first inkling of what might possibly prove a solution of the whole affair.

I wished now that I had encouraged his incoherent ramble of speech, instead of heading him off; but I had done so because I could not bear to have him talk as he had.

Yet, with the little I remembered, I began to shape out a theory. It seemed to me that he might be nursing some idea that he had formed — goodness knows how or when — that his sweetheart (still alive) was aboard some derelict in the midst of an enormous "world," he had termed it, of seaweed.

He might have grown more explicit had I not attempted to reason with him, and so lost the rest.

Yet, remembering back, it seemed to me that he must undoubtedly have meant the enormous

Sargasso Sea — that great seaweed-laden ocean, vast almost as Continental Europe, and the final resting-place of the Atlantic's wreckage.

Surely, if he proposed any attempt to search through that, then there could be no doubt but that he was temporarily unbalanced. And yet I could do nothing. I was a prisoner and helpless.

IV.

Eight days of variable but strongish winds passed, and still I was a prisoner in my cabin. From the ports that opened out astern and on each side — for my cabin runs right across the whole width of the stern — I was able to command a good view of the surrounding ocean, which now had commenced to be laden with great floating patches of Gulf weed — many of them hundreds and hundreds of yards in length.

And still we held on, apparently towards the nucleus of the Sargasso Sea. This I was able to assume by means of a chart which I had found in one of the lockers, and the course I had been able to gather from the "tell-tale" compass let into the cabin ceiling.

And so another and another day went by, and now we were among weed so thick that at times the vessel found difficulty in forcing her way through, while the surface of the sea had assumed a curious oily appearance, though the wind was still quite strong.

It was later in the day that we encountered a bank of weed so prodigious that we had to up helm and run round it, and after that the same experience was many times repeated; and so the night found us.

The following morning found me at the ports, eagerly peering out across the water. From one of those on the starboard side, I could discern at a considerable distance a huge bank of weed that seemed to be unending, and to run parallel with our broadside. It appeared to rise in places a couple of feet above the level of the surrounding sea.

For a long while I stared, then went across to the port side. Here I found that a similar bank stretched away on our port beam. It was as though we were sailing up an immense river, the low banks of which were formed of seaweed instead of land.

And so that day passed hour by hour, the weedbanks growing more definite and seeming to be nearer. Towards evening something came into sight —a far, dim hulk, the masts gone, the whole hull covered with growth, an unwholesome green, blotched with brown in the light from the dying sun.

I saw this lonesome craft from a port on the starboard side, and the sight roused a multitude of questionings and thoughts.

Evidently we had penetrated into the unknown

central portion of the enormous Sargasso, the Great Eddy of the Atlantic, and this was some lonely derelict, lost ages ago perhaps to the outside world.

Just at the going down of the sun, I saw another; she was nearer, and still possessed two of her masts, which stuck up bare and desolate into the darkening sky. She could not have been more than a quarter of a mile in from the edge of the weed. As we passed her I craned out my head through the port to stare at her. As I stared the dusk grew out of the abyss of the air, and she faded presently from sight into the surrounding loneliness.

Through all that night I sat at the port and watched, listening and peering; for the tremendous mystery of that inhuman weed-world was upon me.

In the air there rose no sound; even the wind was scarcely more than a low hum aloft among the sails and gear, and under me the oily water gave no rippling noise. All was silence, supreme and unearthly.

About midnight the moon rose away on our starboard beam, and from then until the dawn I stared out upon a ghostly world of noiseless weed, fantastic, silent, and unbelievable, under the moonlight.

On four separate occasions my gaze lit on black hulks that rose above the surrounding weeds — the hulks of long-lost vessels. And once, just when the strangeness of dawn was in the sky, a faint, long-drawn wailing seemed to come floating to me across the immeasurable waste of weed.

It startled my strung nerves, and I assured myself that it was the cry of some lone sea bird. Yet, my imagination reached out for some stranger explanation.

The eastward sky began to flush with the dawn, and the morning light grew subtly over the breadth of the enormous ocean of weed until it seemed to me to reach away unbroken on each beam into the grey horizons. Only astern of us, like a broad road of oil, ran the strange river-like gulf up which we had sailed.

Now I noticed that the banks of weed were nearer, very much nearer and a disagreeable thought came to me. This vast rift that had allowed us to penetrate into the very nucleus of the Sargasso Sea — suppose it should close!

It would mean inevitably that there would be one more among the missing — another unanswered mystery of the inscrutable ocean. I resisted the thought, and came back more directly into the present.

Evidently the wind was still dropping, for we were moving slowly, as a glance at the ever-nearing weed-banks told me. The hours passed on, and my breakfast, when the steward brought it, I took to one of the ports, and there ate; for I would lose nothing of the strange surroundings into which we were so steadily plunging.

And so the morning passed.

V.

It was about an hour after dinner that I observed the open channel between the weedbanks to be narrowing almost minute by minute with uncomfortable speed. I could do nothing except watch and surmise.

At times I felt convinced that the immense masses of weed were closing in upon us, but I fought off the thought with the more hopeful one that we were surely approaching some narrowing outlet of the gulf that yawned so far across the seaweed.

By the time the afternoon was half-through, the weed-banks had approached so close that occasional outjutting masses scraped the yacht's sides in passing. It was now with the stuff below my face, within a few feet of my eyes, that I discovered the immense amount of life that stirred among all the hideous waste.

Innumerable crabs crawled among the seaweed, and once, indistinctly, something stirred among the depths of a large outlying tuft of weed. What it was I could not tell, though afterwards I had an idea; but all I saw was something dark and glistening. We were past it before I could see more.

The steward was in the act of bringing in my tea, when from above there came a noise of shouting, and almost immediately a slight jolt. The man put down the tray he was carrying, and glanced at me, with startled expression.

"What is it, Jones?" I questioned.

"I don't know, sir. I expect it's the weed," he replied.

I ran to the port, craned out my head, and looked forward. Our bow seemed to be embedded in a mass of weeds, and as I watched it came further aft.

Within the next five minutes we had driven through it into a circle of sea that was free from the weed. Across this we seemed to drift, rather than sail, so slow was our speed.

Upon its opposite margin we brought up, the vessel swinging broadside on to the weed, being secured thus with a couple of kedges cast from the bows and stern, though of this I was not aware until later. As we swung, and at last I was able from my port to see ahead, I saw a thing that amazed me.

There, not three hundred feet distant across the quaking weed, a vessel lay embedded. She had been a three-master; but of these only the mizzen was standing. For perhaps a minute I stared, scarcely breathing in my exceeding interest.

All around above her bulwarks, to the height of

apparently some ten feet, ran a sort of fencing formed, so far as I could make out, from canvas, rope, and spars. Even as I wondered at the use of such a thing, I heard my chum's voice overhead. He was hailing her:

"Graiken, ahoy!" he shouted. "Graiken, ahoy!"

At that I fairly jumped. Graiken! What could he mean? I stared out of the port. The blaze of the sinking sun flashed redly upon her stern, and showed the lettering of her name and port; yet the distance was too great for me to read.

I ran across to my table to see if there were a pair of binoculars in the drawers. I found one in the first I opened; then I ran back to the port, racking them out as I went. I reached it, and clapped them to my eyes. Yes; I saw it plainly, her name Graiken and her port London.

From her name my gaze moved to that strange fencing about her. There was a movement in the aft part. As I watched a portion of it slid to one side, and a man's head and shoulders appeared.

I nearly yelled with the excitement of that movement. I could scarcely believe the thing I saw. The man waved an arm, and a vague hail reached us across the weed; then he disappeared. A moment later a score of people crowded the opening, and among them I made out distinctly the face and figure of a girl.

"He was right, after all!" I heard myself saying

out loud in a voice that was toneless through very amazement.

In a minute, I was at the door, beating it with my fists. "Let me out, Ned! Let me out!" I shouted.

I felt that I could forgive him all the indignity that I had suffered. Nay, more; in a queer way I had a feeling that it was I who needed to ask *him* for forgiveness. All my bitterness had gone, and I wanted only to be out and give a hand in the rescue.

Yet though I shouted, no one came, so that at last I returned quickly to the port, to see what further developments there were.

Across the weed I now saw that one man had his hands up to his mouth shouting. His voice reached me only as a faint, hoarse cry; the distance was too great for anyone aboard the yacht to distinguish its import.

From the derelict my attention was drawn abruptly to a scene alongside. A plank was thrown down on to the weed, and the next moment I saw my chum swing himself down the side and leap upon it.

I had opened my mouth to call out to him that I would forgive all were I but freed to lend a hand in this unbelievable rescue.

But even as the words formed they died, for though the weed appeared so dense, it was evidently incapable of bearing any considerable weight, and the plank, with Barlow upon it, sank down into the weed almost to his waist.

He turned and grabbed at the rope with both hands, and in the same moment he gave a loud cry of sheer terror, and commenced to scramble up the yacht's side.

As his feet drew clear of the weed I gave a short cry. Something was curled about his left ankle — something oily, supple, and tapered. As I stared another rose up out from the weed and swayed through the air, made a grab at his leg, missed, and appeared to wave aimlessly. Others came towards him as he struggled upwards.

Then I saw hands reach down from above and seize Barlow beneath the arms. They lifted him by main force, and with him a mass of weed that enfolded something leathery, from which numbers of curling arms writhed.

A hand slashed down with a sheath-knife, and the next instant the hideous thing had fallen back among the weed.

For a couple of seconds longer I remained, my head twisted upwards; then faces appeared once more over our rail, and I saw the men extending arms and fingers, pointing. From above me there rose a hoarse chorus of fear and wonder, and I turned my head swiftly to glance down and across that treacherous extraordinary weedworld.

The whole of the hitherto silent surface was all of a move in one stupendous undulation — as though life had come to all that desolation.

The undulatory movement continued, and abruptly, in a hundred places, the seaweed was tossed up into sudden, billowy hillocks. From these burst mighty arms, and in an instant the evening air was full of them, hundreds and hundreds, coming towards the yacht.

"Devil-fishes!" shouted a man's voice from the deck. "Octopuses! My Gord!"

Then I caught my chum shouting.

"Cut the mooring ropes!" he yelled.

This must have been done almost on the instant, for immediately there showed between us and the nearest weed a broadening gap of scummy water.

"Haul away, lads!" I heard Barlow shouting; and the same instant I caught the splash, splash of something in the water on our port side. I rushed across and looked out. I found that a rope had been carried across to the opposite seaweed, and that the men were now warping us rapidly from those invading horrors.

I raced back to the starboard port, and, lo! as though by magic, there stretched between us and the Graiken only the silent stretch of demure weed and some fifty feet of water. It seem inconceivable that it was a covering to so much terror.

And then speedily the night was upon us, hiding all; but from the decks above there commenced a sound of hammering that continued long through-out the night —long after I, weary with my previous night's vigil, had passed into a fitful slumber, broken anon by that hammering above.

VI.

"Your breakfast, Sir," came respectfully enough in the steward's voice; and I woke with a start. Overhead, there still sounded that persistent hammering, and I turned to the steward for an explanation.

"I don't exactly know, sir," was his reply. "It's something the carpenter's doing to one of the lifeboats." And then he left me.

I ate my breakfast standing at the port, staring at the distant Graiken. The weed was perfectly quiet, and we were lying about the center of the little lake.

As I watched the derelict, it seemed to me that I saw a movement about her side, and I reached for the glasses. Adjusting them, I made out that there were several of the cuttlefish attached to her in different parts, their arms spread out almost starwise across the lower portions of her hull.

Occasionally a feeler would detach itself and wave aimlessly. This it was that had drawn my attention. The sight of these creatures, in conjunction with that extraordinary scene the previous evening, enabled me to guess the use of the great screen running about the Graiken. It had obviously

been erected as a protection against the vile inhabitants of that strange weed-world.

From that my thoughts passed to the problem of reaching and rescuing the crew of the derelict. I could by no means conceive how this was to be effected.

As I stood pondering, whilst I ate, I caught the voices of men chaunteying on deck. For a while this continued; then came Barlow's voice shouting orders, and almost immediately a splash in the water on the starboard side.

I poked my head out through the port, and stared. They had got one of the lifeboats into the water. To the gunnel of the boat they had added a superstructure ending in a roof, the whole somewhat resembling a gigantic dog-kennel.

From under the two sharp ends of the boat rose a couple of planks at an angle of thirty degrees. These appeared to be firmly bolted to the boat and the superstructure. I guessed that their purpose was to enable the boat to over-ride the seaweed, instead of ploughing into it and getting fast.

In the stern of the boat was fixed a strong ringbolt, into which was spliced the end of a coil of one-inch Manilla rope. Along the sides of the boat, and high above the gunnel, the superstructure was pierced with holes for oars. In one side of the roof was placed a trapdoor. The idea struck me as wonderfully ingenious, and a very probable solution of the difficulty of rescuing the crew of the Graiken.

A few minutes later one of the men threw over a rope side-ladder, and ran down it on to the roof of the boat. He opened the trap, and lowered himself into the interior. I noticed that he was armed with one of the yacht's cutlasses and a revolver.

It was evident that my chum fully appreciated the difficulties that were to be overcome. In a few seconds the man was followed by four others of the crew, similarly armed; and then Barlow.

Seeing him, I craned out my head as far as possible, and sang out to him.

"Ned! Ned, old man!" I shouted. "Let me come along with you!"

He appeared never to have heard me. I noticed his face, just before he shut down the trap above him. The expression was fixed and peculiar. It had the uncomfortable remoteness of a sleep-walker.

"Confound it!" I muttered, and after that I said nothing; for it hurt my dignity to supplicate before the men.

From the interior of the boat I heard Barlow's voice, muffled. Immediately four oars were passed out through the holes in the sides, while from slots in the front and rear of the superstructure were thrust a couple of oars with wooden chocks nailed to the blades.

These, I guessed, were intended to assist in steering the boat, that in the bow being primarily for pressing down the weed before the boat, so as to allow her to surmount it the more easily.

Another muffled order came from the interior of the queer-looking craft, and immediately the four oars dipped, and the boat shot towards the weed, the rope trailing out astern as it was paid out from the deck above me.

The board-assisted bow of the lifeboat took the weed with a sort of squashy surge, rose up, and the whole craft appeared to leap from the water down in among the quaking mass.

I saw now the reason why the oar-holes had been placed so high. For of the boat itself nothing could be seen, only the upper portion of the super-structure wallowing amid the weed. Had the holes been lower, there would have been no handling the oars.

I settled myself to watch. There was the probability of a prodigious spectacle, and as I could not help, I would, at least, use my eyes.

Five minutes passed, during which nothing happened, and the boat made slow progress towards the derelict. She had accomplished perhaps some twenty or thirty yards, when suddenly from the Graiken there reached my ears a hoarse shout.

My glance leapt from the boat to the derelict. I

saw that the people aboard had the sliding part of the screen to one side, and were waving their arms frantically, as though motioning the boat back.

Amongst them I could see the girlish figure that had attracted my attention the previous evening. For a moment I stared, then my gaze travelled back to the boat. All was quiet.

The boat had now covered a quarter of the distance, and I began to persuade myself that she would get across without being attacked.

Then, as I gazed anxiously, from a point in the weed a little ahead of the boat there came a sudden quaking ripple that shivered through the weed in a sort of queer tremor. The next instant, like a shot from a gun, a huge mass drove up clear through the tangled weed, hurling it in all directions, and almost capsizing the boat.

The creature had driven up rear foremost. It fell back with a mighty splash, and in the same moment its monstrous arms were reached out to the boat. They grasped it, enfolding themselves about it horribly. It was apparently attempting to drag the boat under.

From the boat came a regular volley of revolver shots. Yet, though the brute writhed, it did not relinquish its hold. The shots closed, and I saw the dull flash of cutlass blades. The men were attempting to hack at the thing through the oar-holes, but evidently with little effect.

All at once the enormous creature seemed to make an effort to overturn the boat. I saw the half-submerged boat go over to one side, until it seemed to me that nothing could right it, and at the sight I went mad with excitement to help them.

I pulled my head in from the port, and glanced round the cabin. I wanted to break down the door, but there was nothing with which to do this.

Then my sight fell upon my bunkboard, which fitted into a sliding groove. It was made of teak wood, and very solid and heavy. I lifted it out, and charged the door with the end of it.

The panels split from top to bottom, for I am a heavy man. Again I struck, and drove the two portions of the door apart. I hove down the bunkboard and rushed through.

There was no one on guard; evidently they had gone on deck to view the rescue. The gunroom door was to my right, and I had the key in my pocket.

In an instant, I had it open, and was lifting down from its rack a heavy elephant gun. Seizing a box of cartridges, I tore off the lid, and emptied the lot into my pocket; then I leapt up the companionway on the deck.

The steward was standing near. He turned at my step; his face was white, and he took a couple of paces towards me doubtfully.

"They're — they're — " he began; but I never let him finish.

"Get out of my way!" I roared and swept him to one side. I ran forward.

"Haul in on that rope!" I shouted. "Tail on to it! Are you going to stand there like a lot of owls and see them drown!"

The men only wanted a leader to show them what to do, and, without showing any thought of insubordination, they tacked on to the rope that was fastened to the stern of the boat, and hauled her back across the weed — cuttle-fish and all.

The strain on the rope had thrown her on an even keel again, so that she took the water safely, though that foul thing was sproddled all across her.

" 'Vast hauling!" I shouted. "Get the doc's cleavers, some of you — anything that'll cut!"

"This is the sort, sir!" cried the bo'sun; from somewhere he had got hold of a formidable double-bladed whale lance.

The boat, still under the impetus given by our pull, struck the side of the yacht immediately beneath where I was waiting with the gun. Astern of it towed the body of the monster, its two eyes — monstrous orbs of the Profound — staring out vilely from behind its arms.

I leant my elbows on the rail, and aimed full at the right eye. As I pulled on the trigger one of the great arms detached itself from the boat, and swirled up towards me. There was a thunderous bang as the heavy charge drove its way through that vast eye, and at the same instant something swept over my head.

There came a cry from behind: "Look out, sir!" A flame of steel before my eyes, and a truncated something fell upon my shoulder, and thence to the deck.

Down below, the water was being churned to a froth, and three more arms sprang into the air, and then down among us.

One grasped the bo'sun, lifting him like a child. Two cleavers gleamed, and he fell to the deck from a height of some twelve feet, along with the severed portion of the limb.

I had my weapons reloaded again by now, and ran forward along the deck somewhat, to be clear of the flying arms that flailed on the rails and deck.

I fired again into the hulk of the brute, and then again. At the second shot, the murderous din of the creature ceased, and, with an ineffectual flicker of its remaining tentacles, it sank out of sight beneath the water.

A minute later we had the hatch in the roof of the superstructure open, and the men out, my chum coming last. They had been mightily shaken, but otherwise were none the worse.

As Barlow came over the gangway, I stepped up to him and gripped his shoulder. I was strangely muddled in my feelings. I felt that I had no sure position aboard my own yacht. Yet all I said was:

"Thank God, you're safe, old man!" And I meant it from my heart.

He looked at me in a doubtful, puzzled sort of manner, and passed his hand across his forehead.

"Yes," he replied; but his voice was strangely toneless, save that some puzzledness seemed to have crept into it. For a couple of moments he stared at me in an unseeing way, and once more I was struck by the immobile, tensed-up expression of his features.

Immediately afterwards he turned away — having shown neither friendliness nor enmity — and commenced to clamber back over the side into the boat.

"Come up, Ned!" I cried. "It's no good. You'll never manage it that way. Look!" and I stretched out my arm, pointing. Instead of looking, he passed his hand once more across his forehead, with that gesture of puzzled doubt. Then, to my relief, he caught at the rope ladder, and commenced to make his way slowly up the side.

Reaching the deck, he stood for nearly a minute without saying a word, his back turned to the derelict. Then, still wordless, he walked slowly across to the opposite side, and leant his elbows upon the rail, as though looking back along the way the yacht had come.

For my part, I said nothing, dividing my attention between him and the men, with occasional glances at the quaking weed and the — apparently — hopelessly surrounded Graiken.

The men were quiet, occasionally turning towards Barlow, as though for some further order. Of me they appeared to take little notice. In this wise, perhaps a quarter of an hour went by; then abruptly Barlow stood upright, waving his arms and shouting:

"It comes! It comes!" He turned towards us, and his face seemed transfigured, his eyes gleaming almost maniacally.

I ran across the deck to his side, and looked away to port, and now I saw what it was that had excited him. The weed-barrier through which we had come on our inward journey was divided, a slowly broadening river of oily water showing clean across it.

Even as I watched it grew broader, the immense masses of weed being moved by some unseen impulsion.

I was still staring, amazed, when a sudden cry went up from some of the men to starboard. Turning quickly, I saw that the yawning movement was being continued to the mass of weed that lay between us and the Graiken.

Slowly, the weed was divided, surely as though an invisible wedge were being driven through it. The gulf of weed-clear water reached the derelict, and passed beyond. And now there was no longer anything to stop our rescue of the crew of the derelict.

VII.

It was Barlow's voice that gave the order for the mooring ropes to be cast off, and then, as the light wind was right against us, a boat was out ahead, and the yacht was towed towards the ship, whilst a dozen of the men stood ready with their rifles on the fo'c's'le head.

As we drew nearer, I began to distinguish the features of the crew, the men strangely grizzled and old looking. And among them, white-faced with emotion, was my chum's lost sweetheart. I never expect to know a more extraordinary moment.

I looked at Barlow; he was staring at the white-faced girl with an extraordinary fixity of expression that was scarcely the look of a sane man.

The next minute we were alongside, crushing to a pulp between our steel sides one of those remaining monsters of the deep that had continued to cling steadfastly to the Graiken.

Yet of that I was scarcely aware, for I had turned again to look at Ned Barlow. He was swaying slowly to his feet, and just as the two vessels closed he reached up both his hands to his head, and fell like a log.

Brandy was brought, and later Barlow carried to his cabin; yet we had won clear of that hideous weed-world before he recovered consciousness.

During his illness I learned from his sweetheart how, on a terrible night a long year previously, the Graiken had been caught in a tremendous storm and dismasted, and how, helpless and driven by the gale, they at last found themselves surrounded by the great banks of floating weed, and finally held fast in the remorseless grip of the dread Sargasso.

She told me of their attempts to free the ship from the weed, and of the attacks of the cuttlefish. And later of various other matters; for all of which I have no room in this story.

In return I told her of our voyage, and her lover's strange behavior. How he had wanted to undertake the navigation of the yacht, and had talked of a great world of weed. How I had — believing him unhinged — refused to listen to him.

How he had taken matters into his own hands, without which she would most certainly have ended her days surrounded by the quaking weed and those great beasts of the deep waters.

She listened with an evergrowing seriousness, so that I had, time and again, to assure her that I bore my old chum no ill, but rather held myself to be in the wrong. At which she shook her head, but seemed mightily relieved.

It was during Barlow's recovery that I made the astonishing discovery that he remembered no detail of his imprisoning of me.

I am convinced now that for days and weeks he

must have lived in a sort of dream in a hyper state, in which I can only imagine that he had possibly been sensitive to more subtle understandings than normal bodily and mental health allows.

One other thing there is in closing. I found that the captain and the two mates had been confined to their cabins by Barlow. The captain was suffering from a pistol-shot in the arm, due to his having attempted to resist Barlow's assumption of authority.

When I released him he vowed vengeance. Yet Ned Barlow being my chum, I found means to slake both the captain's and the two mates' thirst for vengeance, and the slaking thereof is — well, another story.

Eloi Eloi Lama Sabachthani

ELOI ELOI LAMA SABACHTHANI

Dally, Whitlaw and I were discussing the recent stupendous explosion which had occurred in the vicinity of Berlin. We were marvelling concerning the extraordinary period of darkness that had followed, and which had aroused so much newspaper comment, with theories galore.

The papers had got hold of the fact that the War Authorities had been experimenting with a new explosive, invented by a certain chemist, named Baumoff, and they referred to it constantly as "The New Baumoff Explosive".

We were in the Club, and the fourth man at our table was John Stafford, who was professionally a medical man, but privately in the Intelligence Department. Once or twice, as we talked, I had glanced at Stafford, wishing to fire a question at him; for he had been acquainted with Baumoff. But I managed to hold my tongue; for I knew that if I asked out pointblank, Stafford (who's a good sort, but a bit of an ass as regards his almost ponderous code-of-silence) would be just as like as not to say

77

that it was a subject upon which he felt he was not entitled to speak.

Oh, I know the old donkey's way; and when he had once said that, we might just make up our minds never to get another word out of him on the matter, as long as we lived. Yet, I was satisfied to notice that he seemed a bit restless, as if he were on the itch to shove in his oar; by which I guessed that the papers we were quoting had got things very badly muddled indeed, in some way or other, at least as regarded his friend Baumoff. Suddenly, he spoke:

"What unmitigated, wicked piffle!" said Stafford, quite warm. "I tell you it *is* wicked, this associating of Baumoff's name with war inventions and such horrors. He was the most intensely poetical and earnest follower of the Christ that I have ever met; and it is just the brutal Irony of Circumstance that has attempted to use one of the products of his genius for a purpose of Destruction. But you'll find they won't be able to use it, in spite of their having got hold of Baumoff's formula. As an explosive it is not practicable. It is, shall I say, too impartial; there is no way of controlling it.

"I know more about it, perhaps, than any man alive; for I was Baumoff's greatest friend, and when he died, I lost the best comrade a man ever had. I need make no secret about it to you chaps. I was 'on duty' in Berlin, and I was deputed to get in touch with Baumoff. The government had long had an eye on him; he was an Experimental Chemist, you know, and altogether too jolly clever to ignore. But there was no need to worry about him. I got to know him, and we became enormous friends; for I soon found that *he* would never turn his abilities towards any new war-contrivance; and so, you see, I was able to enjoy my friendship with him, with a comfy conscience — a thing our chaps are not always able to do in their friendships. Oh, I tell you, it's a mean, sneaking, treacherous sort of business, ours; though it's necessary; just as some odd man, or other, has to be a hangsman. There's a number of unclean jobs to be done to keep the Social Machine running!

"I think Baumoff was the most enthusiastic *intelligent* believer in Christ that it will be ever possible to produce. I learned that he was compiling and evolving a treatise of most extraordinary and convincing proofs in support of the more inexplicable things concerning the life and death of Christ. He was, when I became acquainted with him, concentrating his attention particularly upon endeavouring to show that the Darkness of the Cross, between the sixth and the ninth hours, was a very real thing, possessing a tremendous significance. He intended at one sweep to smash utterly all talk of a timely thunderstorm or any of the other more or less inefficient theories which have been brought forward from time to time to explain the occurrence away as being a thing of no particular significance.

"Baumoff had a pet aversion, an atheistic Professor of Physics, named Hautch, who — using the 'marvellous' element of the life and death of Christ, as a fulcrum from which to attack Baumoff's theories — smashed at him constantly, both in his lectures and in print. Particularly did he pour bitter unbelief upon Baumoff's upholding that the Darkness of the Cross was anything more than a gloomy hour or two, magnified into blackness by the emotional inaccuracy of the Eastern mind and tongue.

"One evening, some time after our friendship had become very real, I called on Baumoff, and found him in a state of tremendous indignation over some article of the Professor's which attacked him brutally; using his theory of the *Significance* of the 'Darkness', as a target. Poor Baumoff! It was certainly a marvellously clever attack; the attack of a thoroughly trained, well-balanced Logician. But Baumoff was something more; he was Genius. It is a title few have any rights to; but it was his!

"He talked to me about his theory, telling me that he wanted to show me a small experiment, presently, bearing out his opinions. In his talk, he told me several things that interested me extremely. Having first reminded me of the fundamental fact that light is conveyed to the eye through the means of that indefinable medium, named the Aether. He went a step further, and pointed out to me that, from an aspect which more approached the primary,

Light was a vibration of the Aether, of a certain definite number of waves per second, which possessed the power of producing upon our retina the sensation which we term Light.

"To this, I nodded; being, as of course is everyone, acquainted with so well-known a statement. From this, he took a quick, mental stride, and told me that an ineffably vague, but measurable, darkening of the atmosphere (greater or smaller according to the personality-force of the individual) was always evoked in the immediate vicinity of the human, during any period of great emotional stress.

"Step by step, Baumoff showed me how his research had led him to the conclusion that this queer darkening (a million times too subtle to be apparent to the eye) could be produced only through something which had power to disturb or temporally interrupt or break up the Vibration of Light. In other words, there was, at any time of unusual emotional activity, some disturbance of the Aether in the immediate vicinity of the person suffering, which had some effect upon the Vibration of Light, interrupting it, and producing the aforementioned infinitely vague darkening.

" 'Yes?' I said, as he paused, and looked at me, as if expecting me to have arrived at a certain definite deduction through his remarks. 'Go on.'

" 'Well,' he said, 'don't you see, the subtle darkening around the person suffering, is greater or less, according to the personality of the suffering human. Don't you?'

" 'Oh!' I said, with a little gasp of astounded comprehension, 'I see what you mean. You — you mean that if the agony of a person of ordinary personality can produce a faint disturbance of the Aether, with a consequent faint darkening, then the Agony of Christ, possessed of the Enormous Personality of the Christ, would produce a terrific disturbance of the Aether, and therefore, it might chance, of the Vibration of Light, and that this is the true explanation of the Darkness of the Cross; and that the fact of such an extraordinary and apparently unnatural and improbable Darkness having been recorded is not a thing to weaken the Marvel of Christ. But one more unutterably wonderful, infallible proof of His God-like power? Is that it? Is it? Tell me?'

"Baumoff just rocked on his chair with delight, beating one fist into the palm of his other hand, and nodding all the time to my summary. How he *loved* to be understood; as the Searcher always craves to be understood.

" 'And now,' he said, 'I'm going to show you something.'

"He took a tiny, corked test-tube out of his waistcoat pocket, and emptied its contents (which consisted of a single, grey-white grain, about twice the size of an ordinary pin's head) on to his dessert plate. He crushed it gently to powder with the ivory handle of a knife, then damped it gently, with a single minim of what I supposed to be water, and worked it up into a tiny patch of grey-white paste. He then took out his gold tooth-pick, and thrust it into the flame of a small chemist's spirit lamp, which had been lit since dinner as a pipe-lighter. He held the gold tooth-pick in the flame, until the narrow, gold blade glowed whitehot.

" 'Now look!' he said, and touched the end of the tooth-pick against the infinitesmal patch upon the dessert plate. There came a swift little violet flash, and suddenly I found that I was staring at Baumoff through a sort of transparent darkness, which faded swiftly into a black opaqueness. I thought at first this must be the complementary effect of the flash upon the retina. But a minute passed, and we were still in that extraordinary darkness.

" 'My Gracious! Man! What is it?' I asked, at last.

"His voice explained then, that he had produced, through the medium of chemistry, an exaggerated effect which simulated, to some extent, the disturbance in the Aether produced by waves thrown off by any person during an emotional crisis or agony. The waves, or vibrations, sent out by his experiment produced only a partial simulation of the effect he wished to show me — merely the temporary interruption of the Vibration of Light, with the resulting darkness in which we both now sat.

" 'That stuff,' said Baumoff, 'would be a tremendous explosive, under certain conditions.'

I heard him puffing at his pipe, as he spoke, but instead of the glow of the pipe shining out visible and red, there was only a faint glare that wavered and disappeared in the most extraordinary fashion.

" 'My Goodness!' I said, 'when's this going away? And I stared across the room to where the big kerosene lamp showed only as a faintly glimmering patch in the gloom; a vague light that shivered and flashed oddly, as though I saw it through an immense gloomy depth of dark and disturbed water.

" 'It's all right,' Baumoff's voice said from out of the darkness. 'It's going now; in five minutes the disturbance will have quieted, and the waves of light will flow off evenly from the lamp in their normal fashion. But, whilst we're waiting, isn't it immense, eh?'

" 'Yes,' I said. 'It's wonderful; but it's rather unearthly, you know.'

" 'Oh, but I've something much finer to show you,' he said. 'The real thing. Wait another minute. The darkness is going. See! You can see the light from the lamp now quite plainly. It looks as if it were submerged in a boil of waters, doesn't it? that are growing clearer and clearer and quieter and quieter all the time.'

"It was as he said; and we watched the lamp, silently, until all signs of the disturbance of the light-carrying medium had ceased. Then Baumoff faced me once more.

"Now,' he said. 'You've seen the somewhat casual effects of just crude combustion of that stuff of mine. I'm going to show you the effects of combusting it in the human furnace, that is, in my own body; and then, you'll see one of the great wonders of Christ's death reproduced on a miniature scale.'

"He went across to the mantelpiece, and returned with a small, 120 minim glass and another of the tiny, corked test-tubes, containing a single grey-white grain of his chemical substance. He uncorked the test-tube, and shook the grain of substance into the minim glass, and then, with a glass stirring-rod, crushed it up in the bottom of the glass, adding water, drop by drop as he did so, until there were sixty minims in the glass.

" 'Now!' he said, and lifting it, he drank the stuff. 'We will give it thirty-five minutes,' he continued; 'then, as carbonization proceeds, you will find my pulse will increase, as also the respiration, and presently there will come the darkness again, in the subtlest, strangest fashion; but accompanied now by certain physical and psychic phenomena, which will be owing to the fact that the vibrations it will throw off, will be blent into what I might call the emotional-vibrations, which I shall give off in my distress. These will be enormously intensified, and you will possibly experience an extraordinarily interesting demonstration of the soundness of my more theoretical reasonings. I tested it by myself last week' (He waved a bandaged finger at me), 'and I read a paper to the Club on the results. They are very enthusiastic, and have promised their co-operation in the big demonstration I intend to give on next Good Friday — that's seven weeks off, to-day.'

"He had ceased smoking; but continued to talk quietly in this fashion for the next thirty-five minutes. The Club to which he had referred was a peculiar association of men, banded together under the presidentship of Baumoff himself, and having for their appellation the title of — so well as I can translate it —'The Believers And Provers Of Christ'. If I may say so, without any thought of irreverence, they were, many of them, men fanatically crazed to uphold the Christ. You will agree later, I think, that I have not used an incorrect term, in describing the bulk of the members of this extraordinary club, which was, in its way, well worthy of one of the religio-maniacal extrudences which have been forced into temporary being by certain of the more religiously-emotional minded of our cousins across the water.

"Baumoff looked at the clock; then held out his wrist to me. 'Take my pulse,' he said, 'it's rising fast. Interesting data, you know.'

"I nodded, and drew out my watch. I had noticed that his respirations were increasing; and I found his pulse running evenly and strongly at 105. Three minutes later, it had risen to 175, and his respirations to 41. In a further three minutes, I took his pulse again, and found it running at 203, but with the rhythm regular. His respirations were then 49. He had, as I knew, excellent lungs, and his heart was sound. His lungs, I may say, were of exceptional capacity, and there was at this stage no marked dyspnoea. Three minutes later I found the pulse to be 227, and the respiration 54.

" 'You've plenty of red corpuscles, Baumoff!' I said. 'But I hope you're not going to overdo things.'

"He nodded at me, and smiled; but said nothing. Three minutes later, when I took the last pulse, it was 233, and the two sides of the heart were sending out unequal quantities of blood, with an irregular rhythm. The respiration had risen to 67 and was becoming shallow and ineffectual, and dyspnoea was becoming very marked. The small amount of arterial blood leaving the left side of the heart betrayed itself in the curious bluish and white tinge of the face.

" 'Baumoff!' I said, and began to remonstrate; but he checked me, with a queerly invincible gesture.

" 'It's all right!' he said, breathlessly, with a little

note of impatience. 'I know what I'm doing all the time. You must remember I took the same degree as you in medicine.'

"It was quite true. I remembered then that he had taken his M.D. in London; and this in addition to half a dozen other degrees in different branches of the sciences in his own country. And then, even as the memory reassured me that he was not acting in ignorance of the possible danger, he called out in a curious, breathless voice:

" 'The Darkness! It's beginning. Take note of every single thing. Don't bother about me. I'm all right!'

"I glanced swiftly round the room. It was as he had said. I perceived it now. There appeared to be an extraordinary quality of gloom growing in the atmosphere of the room. A kind of bluish gloom, vague, and scarcely, as yet, affecting the transparency of the atmosphere to light.

"Suddenly, Baumoff did something that rather sickened me. He drew his wrist away from me, and reached out to a small metal box, such as one sterilizes a hypodermic in. He opened the box, and took out four rather curious looking drawing-pins, I might call them, only they had spikes of steel fully an inch long, whilst all around the rim of the heads (which were also of steel) there projected downward, parallel with the central spike, a number of shorter spikes, maybe an eighth of an inch long.

"He kicked off his pumps; then stooped and slipped his socks off, and I saw that he was wearing a pair of linen inner-socks.

" 'Antiseptic!' he said, glancing at me. 'Got my feet ready before you came. No use running unnecessary risks.' He gasped as he spoke. Then he took one of the curious little steel spikes.

" 'I've sterilized them,' he said; and therewith, with deliberation, he pressed it in up to the head into his foot between the second and third branches of the dorsal artery.

" 'For God's sake, what are you doing!' I said, half rising from my chair.

" 'Sit down!' he said, in a grim sort of voice. 'I can't have any interference. I want you simply to observe; keep note of *everything*. You ought to thank me for the chance, instead of worrying me, when you know I shall go my own way all the time.'

"As he spoke, he had pressed in the second of the steel spikes up to the hilt in his left instep, taking the same precaution to avoid the arteries. Not a groan had come from him; only his face betrayed the effect of this additional distress.

" 'My dear chap!' he said, observing my upsetness. 'Do be sensible. I know exactly what I'm doing. There simply *must be distress,* and the readiest way to reach that condition is through physical pain.' His speech had becomes a series of spasmodic words, between gasps, and sweat lay in great clear drops upon his lip and forehead. He slipped off his belt and proceeded to buckle it round both the back of his chair and his waist; as if he expected to need some support from falling.

" 'It's wicked!' I said. Baumoff made an attempt to shrug his heaving shoulders, that was, in its way, one of the most piteous things that I have seen, in its sudden laying bare of the agony that the man was making so little of.

"He was now cleaning the palms of his hands with a little sponge, which he dipped from time to time in a cup of solution. I knew what he was going to do, and suddenly he jerked out, with a painful attempt to grin, an explanation of his bandaged finger. He had held his finger in the flame of the spirit lamp, during his previous experiment; but now, as he made clear in gaspingly uttered words, he wished to simulate as far as possible the actual conditions of the great scene that he had so much in mind. He made it so clear to me that we might expect to experience something very extraordinary, that I was conscious of a sense of almost superstitious nervousness.

" 'I wish you wouldn't, Baumoff!' I said.

" 'Don't — be — silly!' he managed to say. But the two latter words were more groans than words; for between each, he had thrust home right to the heads in the palms of his hands the two remaining steel spikes. He gripped his hands shut, with a sort of spasm of savage determination, and I saw the point of one of the spikes break through the back of his hand, between the extensor tendons of the second and third fingers. A drop of blood beaded the point of the spike. I looked at Baumoff's face; and he looked back steadily at me.

" 'No interference,' he managed to ejaculate. 'I've not gone through all this for nothing. I know — what — I'm doing. Look — it's coming. Take note — everything!'

"He relapsed into silence, except for his painful gasping. I realised that I must give way, and I stared round the room, with a peculiar commingling of an almost nervous discomfort and a stirring of very real and sober curiosity.

" 'Oh,' said Baumoff, after a moment's silence, 'something's going to happen. I can tell. Oh, wait —till I — I have my — big demonstration. I'll know — that — brute Hautch."

"I nodded; but I doubt that he saw me; for his eyes had a distinctly in-turned look, the iris was rather relaxed. I glanced away round the room again; there was a distinct occasional breaking up of the light-rays from the lamp, giving a coming-and-going effect.

"The atmosphere of the room was also quite plainly darker — heavy, with an extraordinary *sense* of gloom. The bluish tint was unmistakably more in evidence; but there was, as yet, none of that opacity which we had experienced before, upon simple combustion, except for the occasional, vague coming-and-going of the lamp-light.

"Baumoff began to speak again, getting his words out between gasps. 'Th' — this dodge of mine gets the — pain into the — the — right place. Right association of — of ideas — emotions — for — best —results. You follow me? Parallelising things — as much as — possible. Fixing whole attention — on the — the death scene — '

"He gasped painfully for a few moments. 'We demonstrate truth of — of The Darkening; but — but there's psychic effect to be — looked for, through — results of parallelisation of — conditions. May have extraordinary simulation of — the *actual thing*. Keep note. Keep note.' Then, suddenly, with a clear, spasmodic burst: 'My God, Stafford, keep note of everything. Something's going to happen. Something — wonderful — Promise not — to bother me. I know — what I'm doing.'

"Baumoff ceased speaking, with a gasp, and there was only the labour of his breathing in the quietness of the room. As I stared at him, halting from a dozen things I needed to say, I realised suddenly that I could no longer see him quite plainly; a sort of wavering in the atmosphere, between us, made him seem momentarily unreal. The whole room had darkened perceptibly in the last thirty seconds; and as I stared around, I realised that there was a constant invisible swirl in the fast-deepening, extraordinary blue gloom that seemed now to permeate everything. When I looked at the lamp, alternate flashings of light and blue — darkness followed each other with an amazing swiftness.

" 'My God!' I heard Baumoff whispering in the half-darkness, as if to himself, 'how did Christ bear the nails!'

"I stared across at him, with an infinite discomfort, and an irritated pity troubling me; but I knew it was no use to remonstrate now. I saw him vaguely distorted through the wavering tremble of the atmosphere. It was somewhat as if I looked at him through convolutions of heated air; only there were marvellous waves of blue-blackness making gaps in my sight. Once I saw his face clearly, full of an infinite pain, that was somehow, seemingly, more spiritual than physical, and dominating everything was an expression of enormous resolution and concentration, making the livid, sweat-damp, agonized face somehow heroic and splendid.

"And then, drenching the room with waves and splashes of opaqueness, the vibration of his abnormally stimulated agony finally broke up the vibration of Light. My last, swift glance round, showed me, as it seemed, the invisible aether boiling and eddying in a tremendous fashion; and, abruptly, the flame of the lamp was lost in an extraordinary swirling patch of light, that marked its position for several moments, shimmering and deadening, shimmering and deadening; until, abruptly, I saw neither that glimmering patch of light, nor anything else. I was suddenly lost in a black opaqueness of night, through which came the fierce, painful breathing of Baumoff.

"A full minute passed; but so slowly that, if I had not been counting Baumoff's respirations, I should have said that it was five. Then Baumoff spoke suddenly, in a voice that was, somehow, curiously changed — a certain toneless note in it:

" 'My God!' he said, from out of the darkness, 'what must Christ have suffered!'

"It was in the succeeding silence, that I had the first realisation that I was vaguely afraid; but the feeling was too indefinite and unfounded, and I might say subconscious, for me to face it out. Three minutes passed, whilst I counted the almost desperate respirations that came to me through the darkness. Then Baumoff began to speak again, and still in that peculiarly altering voice:

" 'By Thy Agony and Bloody Sweat,' he muttered. Twice he repeated this. It was plain indeed that he had fixed his whole attention with tremendous intensity, in his abnormal state, upon the death scene.

"The effect upon me of his intensity was interesting and in some ways extraordinary. As well as I could, I analysed my sensations and emotions and general state of mind, and realised that Baumoff was producing an effect upon me that was almost hypnotic.

"Once, partly because I wished to get my level by the aid of a normal remark, and also because I was sud-

denly newly anxious by a change in the breath-
sounds, I asked Baumoff how he was. My voice going
with a peculiar and really uncomfortable blankness
through that impenetrable blackness of opacity.

"He said: 'Hush! I'm carrying the Cross.' And, do
you know, the effect of those simple words, spoken in
that new, toneless voice, in that atmosphere of almost
unbearable tenseness, was so powerful that, suddenly,
with eyes wide open, I saw Baumoff clear and vivid
against that unnatural darkness, carrying a Cross.
Not, as the picture is usually shown of the Christ, with
it crooked over the shoulder; but with the Cross
gripped just under the cross-piece in his arms, and the
end trailing behind, along rocky ground. I saw even
the pattern of the grain of the rough wood, where some
of the bark had been ripped away; and under the trailing end there was a tussock of tough wire-grass, that
had been uprooted by the towing end, and dragged
and ground along upon the rocks, between the end of
the Cross and the rocky ground. I can see the thing
now, as I speak. It's vividness was extraordinary; but it
had come and gone like a flash, and I was sitting there
in the darkness, mechanically counting the respirations; yet unaware that I counted.

"As I sat there, it came to me suddenly — the
whole entire marvel of the thing that Baumoff had
achieved. I was sitting there in a darkness which was
an actual reproduction of the miracle of the Darkness
of the Cross. In short, Baumoff had, by producing in

himself an abnormal condition, developed an Energy of Emotion that must have almost, in its effects, paralleled the Agony of the Cross. And in so doing, he had shown from an entirely new and wonderful point, the indisputable truth of the stupendous personality and the enormous spiritual force of the Christ. He had evolved and made practical to the average understanding a proof that would make to live again the *reality* of that wonder of the world — *CHRIST*. And for all this, I had nothing but admiration of an almost stupefied kind.

"But, at this point, I felt that the experiment should stop. I had a strangely nervous craving for Baumoff to end it right there and then, and not to try to parallel the psychic conditions. I had, even then, by some queer aid of sub-conscious suggestion, a vague reaching-out-towards the danger of "monstrosity" being induced, instead of any actual knowledge gained.

"Baumoff!' I said. 'Stop it!'

"But he made no reply, and for some minutes there followed a silence, that was unbroken, save by his gasping breathing. Abruptly, Baumoff said, between his gasps: 'Woman — behold — thy — son.' He muttered this several times, in the same uncomfortably toneless voice in which he had spoken since the darkness became complete.

" 'Baumoff!' I said again. 'Baumoff! *Stop it!*' And as I listened for his answer, I was relieved to think that his breathing was less shallow. The abnormal demand for oxygen was evidently being met, and the extravagant call upon the heart's efficiency was being relaxed.

" 'Baumoff!' I said, once more. 'Baumoff! Stop it!'"

"And, as I spoke, abruptly, I thought the room was shaken a little.

"Now, I had already as you will have realised, been vaguely conscious of a peculiar and growing nervousness. I think that is the word that best describes it, up to this moment. At this curious little shake that seemed to stir through the utterly dark room, I was suddenly more than nervous. I felt a thrill of actual and literal fear; yet with no sufficient cause of reason to justify me; so that, after sitting very tense for some long minutes, and feeling nothing further, I decided that I needed to take myself in hand, and keep a firmer grip upon my nerves. And then, just as I had arrived at this more comfortable state of mind, the room was shaken again, with the most curious and sickening oscillatory movement, that was beyond all comfort of denial.

" 'My God!' I whispered. And then, with a sudden effort of courage, I called: 'Baumoff! *For God's sake stop it!*'

"You've no idea of the effort it took to speak aloud into that darkness; and when I did speak, the sound of my voice set me afresh on edge. It went so empty and *raw* across the room; and somehow, the room seemed to be incredibly big. Oh, I wonder whether you realise how beastly I felt, without my having to make any further effort to tell you.

"And Baumoff never answered a word; but I could hear him breathing, a little fuller; though still heaving his thorax painfully, in his need for air. The incredible shaking of the room eased away; and there succeeded a spasm of quiet, in which I felt that it was my duty to get up and step across to Baumoff's chair. But I could not do it. Somehow, I would not have touched Baumoff then for any cause whatever. Yet, even in that moment, as now I know, I was not aware that I was *afraid* to touch Baumoff.

"And then the oscillations commenced again. I felt the seat of my trousers slide against the seat of my chair, and I thrust out my legs, spreading my feet against the carpet, to keep me from sliding off one way or the other on to the floor. To say I was afraid, was not to describe my state at all. I was terrified. And suddenly, I had comfort, in the most extraordinary fashion; for a single idea literally glazed into my brain, and gave me a reason to which to cling. It was a single line:

" 'Aether, the soul of iron and sundry stuffs' which Baumoff had once taken as a text for an extraordinary lecture on vibrations, in the earlier days of our friendship. He had formulated the suggestion that, in embryo, Matter was, from a primary aspect, a localised vibration, traversing a closed orbit. These primary localised vibrations were inconceivably minute.

But were capable, under certain conditions, of combining under the action of keynote-vibrations into secondary vibrations of a size and shape to be determined by a multitude of only guessable factors. These would sustain their new form, so long as nothing occurred to disorganise their combination or depreciate or divert their energy — their unity being partially determined by the inertia of the still Aether outside of the closed path which their area of activities covered. And such combination of the primary localised vibrations was neither more nor less than matter. Men and worlds, aye! and universes.

"And then he had said the thing that struck me most. He had said, that if it were possible to produce a vibration of the Aether of a sufficient energy, it would be possible to disorganise or confuse the vibration of matter. That, given a machine capable of creating a vibration of the Aether of a sufficient energy, he would engage to destroy not merely the world, but the whole universe itself, including heaven and hell themselves, if such places existed, and had such existence in a material form.

"I remember how I looked at him, bewildered by the pregnancy and scope of his imagination. And now his lecture had come back to me to help my courage with the sanity of reason. Was it not possible that the Aether disturbance which he had produced, had sufficient energy to cause some disorganisation of the vibration of matter, in the immediate vicinity, and had thus created a miniature quaking of the ground all about the house, and so set the house gently a-shake?

"And then, as this thought came to me, another and a greater, flashed into my mind. 'My God!' I said out loud into the darkness of the room. It explains one more mystery of the Cross, the disturbance of the Aether caused by Christ's Agony, disorganised the vibration of matter in the vicinity of the Cross, and there was then a small local earthquake, which opened the graves, and rent the veil, possibly by disturbing its supports. And, of course, the earthquake was an effect, and *not* a cause, as belittlers of the Christ have always insisted.

" 'Baumoff!' I called. 'Baumoff, you've proved another thing. Baumoff! Baumoff! Answer me. Are you all right?'

"Baumoff answered, sharp and sudden out of the darkness; but not to me:

" 'My God!' he said. 'My God!' His voice came out at me, a cry of veritable mental agony. He was suffering, in some hypnotic, induced fashion, something of the very agony of the Christ Himself.

" 'Baumoff!' I shouted, and forced myself to my feet. I heard his chair clattering, as he sat there and shook. 'Baumoff!'

An extraordinary quake went across the floor of the room, and I heard a creaking of the woodwork, and something fell and smashed in the darkness. Baum-

off's gasps hurt me; but I stood there. I dared not go to him. I knew *then* that I was afraid of him — of his condition, or something I don't know what. But, oh, I was horribly afraid of him.

" 'Bau — ' I began, but suddenly I was afraid even to speak to him. And I could not move. Abruptly, he cried out in a tone of incredible anguish:

" 'Eloi, Eloi, lama sabach*thani!*' But the last word changed in his mouth, from his dreadful hypnotic grief and pain, to a scream of simply infernal terror.

"And, suddenly, a horrible mocking voice roared out in the room, from Baumoff's chair: 'Eloi, Eloi, lama sabachthani!'

"Do you understand, the voice was not Baumoff's at all. It was not a voice of despair; but a voice sneering in an incredible, bestial, monstrous fashion. In the succeeding silence, as I stood in an ice of fear, I knew that Baumoff no longer gasped. The room was absolutely silent, the most dreadful and silent place in all this world. Then I bolted; caught my foot, probably in the invisible edge of the hearth-rug, and pitched headlong into a blaze of internal brain-stars. After which, for a very long time, certainly some hours, I knew nothing of any kind.

"I came back into this Present, with a dreadful headache oppressing me, to the exclusion of all else. But the Darkness had dissipated. I rolled over on to my side, and saw Baumoff and forgot even the pain in my head. He was leaning forward towards me; his eyes wide open, but dull. His face was enormously swollen, and there was, somehow, something *beastly* about him. He was dead, and the belt about him and the chair-back,alone prevented him from falling forward on to me. His tongue was thrust out of one corner of his mouth. I shall always remember how he looked. He was leering, like a human-beast, more than a man.

"I edged away from him, across the floor; but I never stopped looking at him, until I had got to the other side of the door, and closed between us. Of course, I got my balance in a bit, and went back to him; but there was nothing I could do.

"Baumoff died of heart-failure, of course, obviously! I should never be so foolish as to suggest to any sane jury that, in his extraordinary, self-hypnotised, defenseless condition, he was "entered" by some Christ-apeing Monster of the Void. I've too much respect for my own claim to be a common-sensible man, to put forward such an idea with seriousness! Oh, I know I may seem to speak with a jeer; but what can I do but jeer at myself and all the world, when I dare not acknowledge, even secretly to myself, what my own thoughts are. Baumoff did, undoubtedly die of heart-failure; and, for the rest, how much was I hyp-notised into believing. Only, there was over by the far wall, where it had been shaken down to the floor from a solidly fastened-up bracket, a little pile of glass that had once formed a piece of beautiful Venetian glassware. You remember that I heard something fall, when the room shook. Surely the room *did* shake? Oh, I must stop thinking. My head goes round.

"The explosive the papers are talking about. Yes, that's Baumoff's; that makes it all seem true, doesn't it? They had the darkness at Berlin, after the explosion. There is no getting away from *that.* The Government know only that Baumoff's formulae is capable of producing the largest quantity of gas, in the shortest possible time. That, in short, it is ideally *explosive.* So it is; but I imagine it will prove an explosive, as I have already said, and as experience has proved, a little too impartial in its action for it to create enthusiasm on either side of a battlefield. Perhaps this is but a mercy, in disguise; certainly a mercy, if Baumoff's theories as to the possibility of disorganising matter, be anywhere near to the truth.

"I have thought sometimes that there might be a more normal explanation of the dreadful thing that happened at the end. Beaumoff *may* have ruptured a blood-vessel in the brain, owing to the enormous arterial pressure that his experiment induced; and the voice I heard and the mockery and the horrible expression and leer may have been nothing more than the immediate outburst and expression of the natural "obliqueness" of a deranged mind, which so often turns up a side of a man's nature and produces an inversion of character, that is the very complement of

his normal state. And certainly, poor Baumoff's normal religious attitude was one of marvellous reverence
and loyalty towards the Christ.

"Also, in support of this line of explanation, I
have frequently observed that the voice of a person
suffering from mental derangement is frequently
wonderfully changed, and has in it often a very repel-
lant and inhuman quality. I try to think that this
explanation fits the case. But I can never forget that
room. Never."

The Terror Of the Water-Tank

THE TERROR OF THE WATER-TANK

Crowning the heights on the outskirts of a certain town on the east coast is a large, iron water-tank from which an isolated row of small villas obtains its supply. The top of this tank has been cemented, and round it have been placed railings, thus making of it a splendid "look-out" for any of the townspeople who may choose to promenade upon it. And very popular it was until the strange and terrible happenings of which I have set out to tell.

Late one evening, a party of three ladies and two gentlemen had climbed the path leading to the tank. They had dined, and it had been suggested that a promenade upon the tank in the cool of the evening would be pleasant. Reaching the level, cemented surface, they were proceeding across it, when one of the ladies stumbled and almost fell over some object lying near the railings on the town-side.

A match having been struck by one of the men, they discovered that it was the body of a portly old gentleman lying in a contorted attitude and apparently quite dead. Horrified, the two men drew off their fair companions to the nearest of the afore-mentioned houses. Then, in company with a passing policeman, they returned with all haste to the spot.

By the aid of the officer's lantern, they ascertained the grewsome fact that the old gentleman had been strangled. In addition, he was without watch or purse. The policeman was able to identify him as an old, retired mill-owner, living some little distance away at a place named Revenge End.

At this point the little party was joined by a stranger, who introduced himself as Dr. Tointon, adding the information that he lived in one of the villas close at hand, and had run across as soon as he had heard there was something wrong.

Silently, the two men and the policeman gathered round, as with deft, skillful hands the doctor made his short examination.

"He's not been dead more than about half an hour," he said at its completion.

He turned towards the two men.

"Tell me how it happened — all you know?"

They told him the little they knew.

"Extraordinary," said the doctor. "And you saw no one?"

"Not a soul, doctor!"

The medical man turned to the officer.

"We must get him home," he said. "Have you sent for the ambulance?"

"Yes, sir," said the policeman. "I whistled to my mate on the lower beat, and 'e went straight off."

The doctor chatted with the two men, and reminded them that they would have to appear at the inquest.

"It's murder?" asked the younger of them in a low voice.

"Well," said the doctor. "It certainly looks like it."

And then came the ambulance.

At this point, I come into actual contact with the story; for old Mr. Marchmount, the retired mill-owner, was the father of my *fiancee,* and I was at the house when the ambulance arrived with its sad burden.

Dr. Tointon had accompanied it along with the policeman, and under his directions the body was taken upstairs, while I broke the news to my sweetheart.

Before he left, the doctor gave me a rough outline of the story as he knew it. I asked him if he had any theory as to how and why the crime had been committed.

"Well," he said, "the watch and chain are missing, and the purse. And then he has undoubtedly been strangled; though with what, I have been unable to decide."

And that was all he could tell me.

The following day there was a long account in the

Northern Daily Telephone about the "shocking murder."
The column ended, I remember, by remarking that
people would do well to beware, as there were evidently some very desperate characters about, and
added that it was believed the police had a clew.

During the afternoon, I myself went up to the
tank. There was a large crowd of people standing in
the road that runs past at some little distance; but the
tank itself was in the hands of the police officer being
stationed at the top of the steps leading up to it. On
learning my connection with the deceased, he allowed
me up to have a look round.

I thanked him, and gave the whole of the tank a
pretty thorough scrutiny, even to the extent of push-
ing my cane down through lock-holes in the iron manhole lids, to ascertain whether the tank was full or
not, and whether there was room for someone to
hide.

On pulling out my stick, I found that the water
reached to within a few inches of the lid, and that the
lids were securely locked. I at once dismissed a vague
theory that had formed in my mind that there might
be some possibility of hiding within the tank itself and
springing out upon the unwary. It was evidently a
common, brutal murder, done for the sake of my pro-
spective father-in-law's purse and gold watch.

One other thing I noticed before I quitted the
tank top. It came to me as I was staring over the rail at
the surrounding piece of waste land. Yet at the time, I

thought little of it, and attached to it no importance whatever. It was that the encircling piece of ground was soft and muddy and quite smooth. Possibly there was a leakage from the tank that accounted for it. Anyhow, that is how it seemed to be.

"There ain't nothin' much to be seen, sir," volunteered the policeman, as I prepared to descend the steps on my way back to the road.

"No," I said. "There seems nothing of which to take hold."

And so I left him, and went on to the doctor's house. Fortunately, he was in, and I at once told him the result of my investigations. Then I asked him whether he thought that the police were really on the track of the criminal.

He shook his head.

"No," he answered. "I was up there this morning having a look round, and since then, I've been thinking. There are one or two points that completely stump me —points that I believe the police have never even stumbled upon."

Yet, though I pressed him, he would say nothing definite.

"Wait!" was all he could tell me.

Yet I had not long to wait before something further happened, something that gave an added note of mystery and terror to the affair.

On the two days following my visit to the doctor, I was kept busy arranging for the funeral of my *fiancee's* father, and then on the very morning of the funeral came the news of the death of the policeman who had been doing duty on the tank.

From my place in the funeral procession, I caught sight of large local posters announcing the fact in great letters, while the newsboys constantly cried:

> "Terror of the Tank —
> Policeman Strangled."

Yet, until the funeral was over, I could not buy a paper to gather any of the details. When at last I was able, I found that the doctor who had attended him was none other than Tointon, and straightway I went up to his place for such further particulars as he could give.

"You've read the newspaper account?" he asked when I met him.

"Yes," I replied.

"Well, you see," he said, "I was right in saying that the police were off the track. I've been up there this morning, and a lot of trouble I had to be allowed to make a few notes on my own account. Even then it was only through the influence of Inspector Slago with whom I have once or twice done a little investigating. They've two men and a sergeant now on duty to keep people away."

"You've done a bit of detective-work, then?"

"At odd times," he replied.

"And have you come to any conclusion?"

"Not yet."

"Tell me what you know of the actual happening," I said. "The newspaper was not very definite. I'm rather mixed up as to how long it was before they found that the policeman had been killed. Who found him?"

"Well, so far as I have been able to gather from Inspector Slago, it was like this. They had detailed one of their men for duty on the tank until two A.M., when he was to be relieved by the next man. At about a minute or so to two, the relief arrived simultaneously with the inspector, who was going his rounds. They met in the road below the tank, and were proceeding up the little side-lane towards the passage, when, from the top of the tank, they heard someone cry out suddenly. The cry ended in a sort of gurgle, and they distinctly heard something fall with a heavy thud.

"Instantly, the two of them rushed up the passage, which as you know is fenced in with tall, sharp, iron railings. Even as they ran, they could hear the beat of struggling heels on the cemented top of the tank, and just as the inspector reached the bottom of the steps there came a last groan. The following moment they were at the top. The policeman threw the light of his lantern around. It struck on a huddled heap near by the right-hand railings — something limp and inert. They ran to it, and found that it was the dead body of the officer who had been on duty. A hurried examination showed that he had been strangled.

"The inspector blew his whistle, and soon another of the force arrived on the scene. This man they at once dispatched for me, and in the meantime they conducted a rapid but thorough search, which, however, brought to light nothing. This was the more extraordinary in that the murderer must have been on the tank even as they went up the steps."

"Jove!" I muttered. "He must have been quick."

The doctor nodded.

"Wait a minute," he went on, "I've not finished yet. When I arrived I found that I could do nothing; the poor fellow's neck had been literally crushed. The power used must have been enormous.

" 'Have you found anything?' I asked the inspector.

" 'No,' he said, and proceeded to tell me as much as he knew, ending by saying that the murderer, who-ever it was, had got clean away.

" 'But,' I exclaimed, 'he would have to pass you, or else jump the railings. There's no other way.'

" 'That's what he's done.' replied Slago rather testily. 'It's no height.'

" 'Then in that case, inspector.' I answered, 'he's left something by which we may be able to trace him.' "

"You mean the mud round the tank, doctor?" I interrupted.

"Yes," said Doctor Tointon. "So you noticed

that, did you? Well, we took the policeman's lamp, and made a thorough search all round the tank — but the whole of the flat surface of mud-covered ground stretched away smooth and unbroken by even a single footprint!"

The doctor stopped dramatically.

"Good God!" I exclaimed, excitedly. "Then how did the fellow get away?"

Doctor Tointon shook his head.

"That is a point, my dear sir, on which I am not yet prepared to speak. And yet I believe I hold a clew."

"What?" I almost shouted.

"Yes," he replied, nodding his head thoughtfully. "To-morrow I may be able to tell you something."

He rose from his chair.

"Why not now?" I asked, madly curious.

"No," he said, "the thing isn't definite enough yet."

He pulled out his watch.

"You must excuse me now. I have a patient waiting."

I reached for my hat, and he went and opened the door.

"To-morrow," he said, and nodded reassuringly as he shook hands. "You'll not forget."

"Is it likely," I replied, and he closed the door after me.

The following morning I received a note from

him asking me to defer my visit until night, as he would be away from home during the greater portion of the day. He mentioned 9:30 as a possible time at which I might call — any time between then and ten P.M. But I was not to be later than that.

Naturally, feeling as curious as I did, I was annoyed at having to wait the whole day. I had intended calling as early as decency would allow. Still, after that note, there was nothing but to wait.

During the morning, I paid a visit to the tank, but was refused permission by the sergeant in charge. There was a large crowd of people in the road below the tank, and in the little side lane that led up to the railed-in passsage. These, like myself, had come up with the intention of seeing the exact spot where the tragedies had occurred; but they were not allowed to pass the men in blue.

Feeling somewhat cross at their persistent refusal to allow me upon the tank, I turned up the lane, which presently turns off to the right. Here, finding a gap in the wall, I clambered over, and disregarding a board threatening terrors to trespassers, I walked across the piece of waste land until I came to the wide belt of mud that surrounded the tank. Then, skirting the edge of the marshy ground, I made my way round until I was on the town-side of the tank. Below me was a large wall which hid me from those in the road below. Between me and the tank stretched some forty feet of smooth, mud-covered earth. This I proceeded now to examine carefully.

As the doctor had said, there was no sign of any footprint in any part of it. My previous puzzlement grew greater. I think I had been entertaining an idea somewhere at the back of my head that the doctor and the police had made a mistake — perhaps missed seeing the obvious, as is more possible than many think. I turned to go back, and at the same moment, a little stream of water began to flow from a pipe just below the edge of the tank top. It was evidently the "overflow." Undoubtedly the tank was brim full.

How, I asked myself, had the murderer got away without leaving a trace?

I made my way back to the gap, and so into the lane. And then, even as I sprang to the ground, an idea came to me — a possible solution of the mystery.

I hurried off to see Dufirst, the tank-keeper, who I knew lived in a little cottage a few hundred feet distant. I reached the cottage, and knocked. The man himself answered me, and nodded affably.

"What an ugly little beast!" I thought. Aloud, I said: "Look here, Dufirst, I want a few particulars about the tank. I know you can tell me what I want to know better than anyone else."

The affability went out of the man's face. "Wot do yer want to know?" he asked surlily.

"Well," I replied. "I want to know if there is any place about the tank where a man could hide."

The fellow looked at me darkly. "No," he said shortly.

"Sure?" I asked.

"Course I am," was his sullen reply.

"There's another thing I want to know about," I went on. "What's the tank built upon?"

"Bed er cerment," he answered.

"And the sides — how thick are they?"

"About 'arf-inch iron."

"One thing more," I said, pulling half-a-crown from my pocket (where-at I saw his face light up). "What are the inside measurements of the tank?" I passed him over the coin.

He hesitated a moment; then slipped it into his waistcoat-pocket. "Come erlong a minnit. I 'ave ther plan of ther thing upstairs, if yer'll sit 'ere an' wait."

"Right," I replied, and sat down, while he disappeared through a door, and presently I heard him rummaging about overhead.

"What a sulky beast," I thought to myself. Then, as the idea passed through my mind, I caught sight of an old bronze luster jug on the opposite side of the room. It stood on a shelf high up; but in a minute I was across the room and reaching up to it; for I have a craze for such things.

"What a beauty," I muttered, as I seized hold of the handle. "I'll offer him five dollars for it."

I had the thing in my hands now. It was heavy. "The old fool!" thought I. "He's been using it to stow odds and ends in." And with that, I took it across to the window. There, in the light, I glanced inside — and nearly dropped it; for within a few inches of my eyes, reposed the old gold watch and chain that had belonged to my murdered friend. For a moment, I felt dazed. Then I knew.

"The little fiend!" I said. "The vile little murderer!"

I put the jug down on the table, and ran to the door. I opened it and glanced out. There, not thirty paces distant was Inspector Slago in company with a constable. They had just gone past the house, and were evidently going up on to the tank.

I did not shout; to do so would have been to warn the man in the room above. I ran after the inspector and caught him by the sleeve.

"Come here, inspector," I gasped. "I've got the murderer."

He twirled round on his heel. "What?" he almost shouted.

"He's in there," I said. "It's the tank-keeper. He's still got the watch and chain. I found it in a jug."

At that the inspector began to run towards the cottage, followed by myself and the policeman. We ran in through the open door, and I pointed to the jug. The inspector picked it up, and glanced inside.

He turned to me. "Can you identify this?" he asked, speaking in a quick, excited voice.

"Certainly I can," I replied. "Mr. Marchmount was to have been my father-in-law. I can swear to the watch being his."

At that instant there came a sound of footsteps on

the stairs and a few seconds later the black bearded little tank-keeper came in through an inner door. In his hand he held a roll of paper — evidently the plan of which he had spoken. Then, as his eyes fell on the inspector holding the watch of the murdered man, I saw the fellow's face suddenly pale.

He gave a sort of little gasp, and his eyes flickered round the room to where the jug had stood. Then he glanced at the three of us, took a step backwards, and jumped for the door through which he had entered. But we were too quick for him, and in a minute had him securely handcuffed.

The inspector warned him that whatever he said would be used as evidence; but there was no need, for he spoke not a word.

"How did you come to tumble across this?" asked the inspector, holding up the watch and guard. "What put you on to it?"

I explained and he nodded.

"It's wonderful," he said. "And I'd no more idea than a mouse that it was him;" nodding towards the prisoner.

Then they marched him off.

That night, I kept my appointment at the doctor's. He had said that he would be able to say something; but I rather fancied that the boot was going to prove on the other leg. It was I who would be able to tell him a great deal more than "something." I had solved the whole mystery in a single morning's work. I rubbed my hands, and wondered what the doctor would have to say in answer to my news. Yet, though I waited until 10:30, he never turned up, so that I had at last to leave without seeing him.

The next morning, I went over to his house. There his housekeeper met me with a telegram that she had just received from a friend of his away down somewhere on the South coast. It was to say that the doctor had been taken seriously ill, and was at present confined to his bed, and was unconscious.

I returned the telegram and left the house. I was sorry for the doctor; but almost more so that I was not able personally to tell him the news of my success as an amateur detective.

It was many weeks before Dr. Tointon returned, and in the meantime the tank-keeper had stood his trial and been condemned for the murder of Mr. Marchmount. In court he had made an improbable statement that he had found the old gentleman dead, and that he had only removed the watch and purse from the body under a momentary impulse. This, of course, did him no good, and when I met the doctor on the day of his return, it wanted only three days to the hanging.

"By the way, doctor," I said, after a few minutes' conversation, "I suppose you know that I spotted the chap who murdered old Mr. Marchmount and the policeman?"

For answer the doctor turned and stared.

"Yes," I said, nodding, "it was the little brute of a tank-keeper. He's to be hanged in three days' time."

"What — " said the doctor, in a startled voice. "Little black Dufirst?"

"Yes," I said, yet vaguely damped by his tone.

"Hanged!" returned the doctor. "Why the man's as innocent as you are!"

I stared at him.

"What do you mean?" I asked. "The watch and chain were found in his possession. They proved him guilty in court."

"Good heavens!" said the doctor. "What awful blindness!"

He turned on me "Why didn't you write and tell me?"

"You were ill — afterwards I thought you'd be sure to have read about it in one of the papers."

"Haven't seen one since I've been ill," he replied sharply. "By George! You've made a pretty muddle of it. Tell me how it happened."

This I did, and he listened intently.

"And, in three days he's to be hanged?" he questioned when I had made an end.

I nodded.

He took off his hat and mopped his face and brow.

"It's going to be a job to save him," he said slowly. "Only three days. My God!"

He looked at me, and then abruptly asked a foolish question.

"Have there been any more — murders up there while I've been ill?" He jerked his hand toward the tank.

"No," I replied. "Of course not. How could there be when they've got the chap who did them!"

He shook his head.

"Besides," I went on, "no one ever goes up there now, at least, not at night, and that's when the murders were done."

"Quite so, quite so," he agreed, as if what I had said fell in with something that he had in his mind.

He turned to me. "Look here," he said, "come up to my place to-night about ten o'clock, and I think I shall be able to prove to you that the thing which killed Marchmount and the policeman was not — well, it wasn't little black Dufirst."

I stared at him.

"Fact," he said.

He turned and started to leave me.

"I'll come," I called out to him.

At the time mentioned, I called at Dr. Tointon's. He opened the door himself and let me in, taking me into his study. Here, to my astonishment, I met Inspector Slago. The inspector wore rather a worried look, and once when Tointon had left the room for a minute, he bent over towards me.

"He seems to think," he said in a hoarse whisper,

and nodding towards the doorway through which the doctor had gone, "that we've made a silly blunder and hooked the wrong man."

"He'll find he's mistaken," I answered.

The inspector looked doubtful, and seemed on the point of saying something further, when the doctor returned.

"Now then," Dr. Tointon remarked, "we'll get ready. Here," he tossed me a pair of rubbers, "shove those on.

"You've got rubber heels, inspector?"

"Yes, sir," replied Slago. "Always wear 'em at night."

The doctor went over to a corner and returned with a double-barreled shotgun which he proceeded to load. This accomplished, he turned to the inspector.

"Got your man outside?"

"Yes, sir," replied Slago.

"Come along, then, the two of you."

We rose and followed him into the dark hall and then out through the front doorway into the silent road. Here we found a plain-clothes policeman waiting, leaning up against a wall. At a low whistle from the inspector, he came swiftly across and saluted. Then the doctor turned and led the way towards the tank.

Though the night was distinctly warm, I shuddered. There was a sense of danger in the air that got on one's nerves. I was quite in the dark as to what was going to happen. We reached the lower end of the

railed passage. Here the doctor halted us, and began
to give directions.

"You have your lantern, inspector?"

"Yes, sir."

"And your man, has he?"

"Yes, sir," replied the man for himself.

"Well, I want you to give yours to my friend for
the present."

The man in plain-clothes passed me his lantern,
and waited further commands.

"Now," said Dr. Tointon, facing me, "I want you
and the inspector to take your stand in the left-hand
corner of the tank top, and have your lanterns ready,
and mind, there must not be a sound, or everything
will be spoiled."

He tapped the plain-clothes man on the shoulder. "Come along," he said.

Reaching the tank top, we took up positions as he
had directed, while he went over with the inspector's
man to the far right-hand corner. After a moment, he
left the officer, and I could just make out the figure of
the latter leaning negligently against the railings.

The doctor came over to us, and sat down
between us.

"You've put him just about where our man was
when we found him," said the inspector in a whisper.

"Yes," replied Dr. Tointon. "Now, listen, and
then there mustn't be another sound. It's a matter of
life and death."

His manner and voice were impressive. "When I

call out 'ready,' throw the light from your lanterns on the officer as smartly as you can. Understand?"

"Yes," we replied together, and after that no one spoke.

The doctor lay down between us on his stomach, the muzzle of his gun directed a little to the right of where the other man stood. Thus we waited. Half an hour passed — an hour, and a sound of distant bells chimed up to us from the valley; then the silence resumed sway. Twice more the far-off bells told of the passing hours, and I was getting dreadfully cramped with staying in one position.

Then abruptly, from somewhere across the tank there came a slight, very slight, slurring, crawling sort of noise. A cold shiver took me, and I peered vainly into the darkness till my eyes ached with the effort. Yet I could see nothing. Indistinctly, I could see the lounging figure of the constable. He seemed never to have stirred from his original position.

The strange rubbing, slurring sound continued. Then came a faint clink of iron, as if someone had kicked against the padlock that fastened down the iron trap over the manhole. Yet it could not be the policeman, for he was not near enough. I saw Dr. Tointon raise his head and peer keenly. Then he brought the butt of his gun up to his shoulder.

I got my lantern ready. I was all tingling with fear and expectation. What was going to happen? There came another slight clink, and then, suddenly, the rustling sound ceased.

I listened breathlessly. Across the tank, the hitherto silent policeman stirred almost, it seemed to me, as if someone or something had touched him. The same instant, I saw the muzzle of the doctor's gun go up some six inches. I grasped my lantern firmly, and drew in a deep breath.

"Ready!" shouted the doctor.

I flashed the light from my lantern across the tank simultaneously with the inspector. I have a confused notion of a twining brown thing about the rail a yard to the right of the constable. Then the doctor's gun spoke once — twice, and it dropped out of sight over the edge of the tank. In the same instant the constable slid down off the rail on to the tank top.

"My God!" shouted the inspector, "has it done for him?"

The doctor was already beside the fallen man, busy loosening his clothing.

"He's all right," he replied. "He's only fainted. The strain was too much. He was a plucky devil to stay. That thing was near him for over a minute."

From somewhere below us in the dark there came a thrashing, rustling sound. I went to the side and threw the light from my lantern downwards. It showed me a writhing yellow something, like an eel or a snake, only the thing was flat like a ribbon. It was twining itself into knots. It had no head. That portion of it seemed to have been blown clean away.

"He'll do now," I heard Dr. Tointon say, and the next instant he was standing beside me. He pointed

downwards at the horrid thing. "There's the murderer," he said.

It was a few evenings later, and the inspector and
I were sitting in the doctor's study.

"Even now, doctor," I said. "I don't see how on
earth you got at it."

The inspector nodded a silent agreement.

"Well," replied Dr. Tointon, "after all it was not
so very difficult. Had I not been so unfortunately
taken ill while away, I should have cleared the
matter up a couple of months ago. You see, I had
exceptional opportunities for observing things, and
in both cases I was very soon on the spot. But all the
same, it was not until the second death occurred that
I knew that the deed was not due to a human hand.
The fact that there were no footprints in the mud
proved that conclusively, and having disposed of
that hypothesis, my eyes were open to take in details
that had hitherto seemed of no moment. For one
thing, both men were found dead almost in the same
spot, and that spot is just over the over-flow pipe."

"It came out of the tank?" I questioned.

"Yes," replied Dr. Tointon. "Then on the
railings near where the thing had happened, I found
traces of slime; and another matter that no one but
myself seems to have been aware of, the collar of the
policeman's coat was wet, and so was Mr. Marchmount's. Lastly, the shape of the marks upon the
necks, and the tremendous force applied, indicated

to me the kind of thing for which I must look. The rest was all a matter of deduction.

"Naturally, all the same, my ideas were somewhat hazy; yet before I saw the brute, I could have told you that it was some form of snake or eel, and I could have made a very good guess at its size. In the course of reasoning the matter out, I had occasion to apply to little black Dufirst. From him, I learned that the tank was supposed to be cleaned out annually, but that in reality it had not been seen to for some years."

"What about Dufirst?" I asked.

"Well," said Dr. Tointon dryly, "I understand he is to be granted a free pardon. Of course the little beast stole those things; but I fancy he's had a fair punishment for his sins."

"And the snake, doctor?" I asked. "What was it?"

He shook his head. "I cannot say," he explained. "I have never seen anything just like it. It is one of those abnormalities that occasionally astonish the scientific world. It is a creature that has developed under abnormal conditions, and, unfortunately, it was so shattered by the heavy charges of shot, that the remains tell me but little — its head, as you saw, was entirely shot away."

I nodded. "It's queer — and frightening," I replied. "Makes a chap think a bit."

"Yes," agreed the doctor. "It certainly ought to prove a lesson in cleanliness."

The Albatross

THE ALBATROSS

I.

"Confound that brute!" I shouted in sheer desperation. Then I sang out to the 'prentice who was keeping "time" on the lee side of the poop, to bring me a piece of spun-yarn and a marlinspike.

I was first mate of the *Skylark,* full-rigged ship, and we were off the Horn on a cold, absolutely windless night. It was the twelve to four watch in the early morning, and four bells (two o'clock) had just gone.

All the watch there had been an enormous albatross flying round and round the vessel; sometimes he would actually fly across the decks, which is a thing I have never known to happen before.

When the boy brought the marlinspike and the yarn, I bent on about two fathoms of the latter, so that I had a sort of handy little harpoon. Then I slipped quickly up the mizzen rigging and out on to the cross-jack yard, where I waited with the spike ready in one hand and the end of the line held fast in the other.

Presently, away forward in the still night, I heard the dismal *squark* of the great bird, and immediately a spate of blasphemy from the man on the lookout, who was evidently getting as much bothered as I by the actions of the creature.

Not a sound then for maybe ten minutes; and then suddenly I saw something float between me and the dim sky-line and come inboard. I lost it for a moment; but immediately there came the loud, dismal *squark* out of the night to my left, and directly afterward I saw vaguely that something was passing under the yard. I raised the marlinspike and drove down at the thing with all my strength, letting the line fly out to its full length. There was a rustle of feathers and a tugging on the line, and the bird *squarked* twice. Then a jerk and the snap of something breaking, and the great albatross was gone free.

I hauled in on the spun-yarn until I had the marlinspike again in my hand; as I passed it between my fingers I felt that there was something caught round the butt, something that felt like a piece of rag. I loosed it from the spike. Then I went down again on to the poop, and at once to the light of the main binnacle, to see what it was that had got caught round the marlinspike. I could not see the thing very plainly at first, and I took the lamp out of the holder, so as to have a better light. I found then that it was a strip of red silk, such as might be torn from a girl's blouse. At one end was a piece of broken tape. For some minutes I examined the thing very carefully. It was in this way that I found presently a single long hair, tangled in the knot of the tape. I picked it loose, gently, and looked at it; then I coiled it round and round my forefinger. It was a girl's hair, brown, with a glint of gold in it! What did it mean? We were off Cape Horn — one of the grim, lonely places of the ocean!

After a while I replaced the lamp in the binnacle and resumed my ordinary tramp of the weather-side of the poop. All the while I was turning this matter over in my brain, and presently I went back again to the light, so that I might have another look at the piece of silk. I saw then that it could not have been very long since it had been torn; for it was very little frayed at the tear and had no appearance of having been weatherworn for more than a few days. Also, the material was new and seemed to be of very fine quality. I grew more puzzled.

Of course it was possible that there was another sailing-ship within a hundred miles of us; it was also possible that such a vessel had a girl aboard, perhaps the captain's daughter; it was also possible that they had caught this particular albatross on a line and tied the silk to it and let it go again. But it was also exceedingly improbable. For sailors will always keep an albatross for the sake of the wing-bones, which make pipe-stems, and the webs, which make purses, and the breast, which makes a gorgeous fire-screen; while others prize the great bill and the beautiful wing-tips.

Moreover, even if the bird had been loosed, why had some one torn up a new silk garment, when a piece of old bunting would have done just as well? You can see how my thoughts were trending. That piece of silk and that long pretty hair coming to me suddenly out of the night in that lonely and desolate sea had stirred me with vague wonderings. Yet I never put my wonderments actually into words, but went back to my constant pacing fore and aft. And so, presently, the second mate came up at eight bells to relieve me.

The next day, through all the eight to twelve forenoon watch, I kept a pretty keen lookout for albatross, but the whole sea was lonely, and though there was such an absolute calm, there was not even a Mother Carey's chicken in sight — only everywhere, so far as the sight might reach, an everlasting gray desolation of water.

The afternoon watch I went below for a sleep. Then, in the first dog-watch, a little before three bells, I saw a great albatross swing and glide against the gray of the sky, about a mile astern. I reached for my glasses and had a good look. I saw the bird plainly, a huge, bony-shouldered albatross, with a queer bulge below the breast. As I stared at him, I grew suddenly excited, for I saw that the bulge was really a packet of some kind tied on to the creature, and there was something fluttering from it.

In the second dog-watch, I asked two of my 'prentices to come down with me into the sail-locker and help me root out an old seine-net that we carried for occasional sport. I told them I was going to have a try for the big albatross that night, if he started flying across the decks again, and they were nearly as keen as I, though I had asked them to do this sail-tossing in their watch below.

When my watch came, from eight until midnight, I did nothing until the "Old Man" had turned in for the night; then I had my boys rig lines for the big net from the main and the mizzen masts, so that we could hoist it up at any moment and let it hang like a curtain between the masts.

The night was very quiet and dark, and though it was difficult to see anything, it would have been easy to hear the bird at a great distance. Yet for over an hour after this there was no sign of anything, and I began to think that we were not to have a visit.

However, just after four bells had gone (ten o'clock) there came from far away over the sea the strange lonely *squark, squark* of an albatross, and a few minutes later I had a vague glimpse of him flying silently round and round the ship, in the way common enough with his kind. Presently he gave out a loud *squark* and turned inboard to fly over the poop.

The next instant there was a loud *squarking* up in the night, and a constant beating of heavy wings. I shouted to the boys at the lines to lower away, and a moment later I was shining the binnacle light on a fluster of beating wings and tangled net.

I sang out to the nearest 'prentice to hold the lamp while I disentangled the albatross and found out what the package was that was made fast to him. The parcel was done up in layer after layer of oilskin, and from the outside there was another such streamer of red silk as the one that had caught on my spike the night before. Then I had come to the last of the wrappings of oilskin and there were a couple of pages torn from a log-book and folded very tight and compact. I opened them, and found that they were covered with hasty feminine handwriting. And this is what I read:

This is written aboard the *Unicorn,* derelict, on the twenty-first day of March, 1904. She was run down by an unknown steamer ten days ago. I am here alone, living in the chart-house. I have food and water sufficient to last me for about a week longer, if I am very careful. The vessel seems to be floating with her decks just a little above the water, and every time the sea is a bit rough it just pours aboard of her.

I am sending this message tied round

the neck of an albatross. The Captain shot
it the day before we were run down, and
hurt the poor creature's wing. I told him he
was an inhuman brute. I am sorry now, for
he, along with every other soul, is dead,
drowned. He was a brave man. The men
crowded into the boats, and he stood with
his revolver and tried to stop them, saying
that no one should leave the ship before I
was safe. He shot two of them, but the others threw him into the sea. They were mad.
They took the boats and went away; and
my maid went with them. But it was
terribly rough, and I saw them sink just a
little way from the ship.

I have been alone ever since, except for
the albatross. I have nursed it, and now it
seems as if it should be able to fly. I pray
God that this message be found before it is
too late! If any find it, come and save a girl
from an awful and lonely death. The position of the ship is written down in the log-
book here in the chart-house, so I will give
it; then you will know where to search for
me. It is Latitude 62° 7′ S. and Longitude
67° 10′ W.

I have sent other messages corked up
in bottles; but this is the one in which I
have all my hope. I shall tie a piece of some-

thing red to it, so that any one seeing my albatross will know it is carrying something and try to catch it. Come, come, come, as quickly as ever you can!

There are enormous numbers of rats about. I suppose the water has driven them up out of the holds and places; but they make me afraid to sleep. Remember, the food I have won't last more than a week, and I am here all alone. But I will be brave. Only don't give up searching for me. The wind has been blowing from the north ever since the night when the boats sank. It is quite calm now. Perhaps these things will help you to know where to look for me, as I can see that the wind must make the ship drift. Don't give me up! Remember I'm waiting, waiting, and trying to be brave.

Mary Doriswold.

You can imagine how I felt, when I had finished reading this paper. Our position that day was 58°S. and 67°30′W.; so that we were at least two hundred and fifty miles to the north of the place where the derelict had been eighteen days earlier; for it was now the twenty-ninth day of March. And there, somewhere away to the southward of us, a girl was dying of hunger and lonesomeness! And there was absolutely no sign of wind.

After a little while I told the boys to clear away the net and take the albatross down on to the main deck and tie it to one of the ring-bolts. Then I took a turn or two up and down the poop, and finally decided to go down and call the "Old Man" and set the matter before him.

When he had heard what I had to tell, he slipped into his clothes and came out into the saloon, where he read the letter twice, very carefully. Then he had a look at the barometer, and afterward came up with me on to the poop and had a look at the weather; but there were certainly no immediate signs of wind.

Through all the rest of the watch he walked up and down with me, discussing the thing, and went several times to the binnacle to make fresh examinations of the letter. Once I suggested the possibility of manning one of the life-boats and trying down to the southward, letting the ship follow on so soon as the wind came. But, of course, he would not listen to this, and very rightly, too. For not only would it have been to risk the lives of all who went in the boat, but to risk the vessel also, because we should have had to leave her undermanned. And so the only thing we could do was to pray for wind.

Down on the main deck I could hear presently the murmur of voices, and I knew that the men had got the news and were talking it over; but that was all that we could do.

At midnight, when the second mate came up to relieve me, he had already learned the story from the 'prentice who called him, and when finally I went below, he and the Skipper were still discussing it.

At four o'clock, when I was waked, my first inquiry was about the wind; but there was not a sign, and when I got on the poop I could see that the weather still had the same dead, settled look.

All that day we kept waiting for the wind that never came; and at last a deputation of the men came aft to ask to be allowed to volunteer to man one of the life-boats and make a search party. But the Master sent them forward again, quietly enough, and even took the trouble to point out the hopelessness of such an attempt, as well as the tremendous risk. For if the derelict were still above water, she might have drifted sufficiently far to be still lost after weeks of searching in the great unknown seas to the southward.

All that day the wind never came, and all that day there was nothing else talked about aboard except the chances of saving the girl. And when at last night came I do not believe half the watch below turned in, but paced the decks, whistling for wind and watching the weather.

The morning came, and still the calm; and at last I asked the Captain whether he would give me permission to take the little gig, which was a light and handy boat, and make the trial alone. I said that if I failed, and the boat was lost, her value would be amply covered by the wages due to me. But the "Old Man" simply refused to listen to the idea, and told me, kindly enough, that it was madness.

I saw that it was no use arguing with him, for he was perfectly right in what he said; but at the same time I was determined to try, if the wind did not come by the evening. For I could not get the thought of that lonely unknown girl out of my mind, and I kept remembering what she had said about the rats.

II.

That night, when the Captain had gone below, I had a talk with the steward, and afterward I gave orders to get the little gig quietly into the water. I provisioned her thoroughly and added a bottle of brandy and a bottle of rum. The second mate fitted her with a boat's compass and binnacle from one of the life-boats, and also attended to the filling of the water-breakers, and saw that all the gear was in place. Then I added my oilskins, some rugs and canvas, and my sextant and chronometer and charts, and so forth. At the last I remembered my shotgun, and ran down for this and plenty of cartridges; for there was no saying how useful it might be.

I shook hands with the second mate, when I returned, and went down into the boat.

"We'll be after you as soon as the wind comes," he said quietly. "Good luck!"

I nodded, and afterward mentioned one or two details of ship's work which would need attention. Then I pulled in the painter and pushed off. As I cleared the side of the vessel, there came a hushed cheering, and hoarse whispers of, "Good luck, sir! Good luck, sir!"

The lamp in the little binnacle was lit, and I turned the hood round, so that I could watch the compass as I pulled. Then I settled down to my work at the oars, and presently the vessel had faded away from me into the night, though for a long while there would come over the sea to me the odd rustle and flap of a sail, as the ship lifted to the occasional glassy swell. But afterward I rowed on through an ever-lasting silence toward the south.

Twice in the night I ceased work, and ate and drank; then onward again, keeping to an easy, regular pull that I knew I could keep up hour after hour.

In the morning I had a good look round, but the *Skylark* was lost below the horizon astern, and the whole world seemed empty. It was a most extraordinary and depressing sensation. I had an early breakfast, and rowed on. Later, I got my longitude; at midday I took my altitude and found that I had done nearly fifty miles to the south.

All that day I pulled steadily, stopping only to eat and drink at regular intervals. That night I slept for six hours, from twelve until six, and when I waked there was still the everlasting calm.

Four more days and nights I went onward in this fashion. All the fourth day I pulled steadily, stopping every half-hour to take a look round; but there was always and only the gray emptiness of the sea. All that night I drifted; for I had passed over, and was now to the southward of, the position of the derelict given by the girl, and I dared not row in the darkness, for fear of passing the wreck.

Part of the night I used in making calculations, and afterward had a good long sleep. I was wakened in the dawn by the lapping of water against the boat, and found that a light breeze had sprung up from the west. This cheered me immensely for I knew that now the *Skylark* would be able to follow, provided that the wind was not merely a local breeze. And, in any case, there was no longer need to use the oars, for I had a mast and sail in the boat.

I stepped the mast and hoisted the lug-sail; then I shipped the rudder and sat down to rest and steer. And it is impossible to express my gratitude; for my hands were raw with broken blisters, and I ached in all my body with the constant and weary labor at the oars.

All that day I ran to the southward, keeping a lookout; but never a sign was there of anything, so that an utter dismay began to come down on me. Yet I did not give up hoping. That night I made fresh calculations, with the result that next morning, as soon as I had hoisted the sail (for I had let the boat drift during the darkness), I altered my course a few degrees to the eastward. At noon I found that I was a hundred and twenty-seven miles to the south and forty-six miles to the east of the last known position of the *Unicorn*. If I sighted nothing by evening, I would make a long tack next day to the north, a few miles eastward of my downward run.

I ran on until the dusk came; and then, after a final long look round, I dropped my sail for the night and set the boat to ride by the painter to a couple of oars, as I had done on the previous nights of drifting.

I felt desperately disheartened, and began to realize more thoroughly my own position, over four hundred miles from the *Skylark* and in a latitude of hopeless and weary storms and utterly unfrequented by ships. Yet I fought this down and finally settled myself to sleep, well wrapped up in my rugs, for it was bitterly cold, though so fine.

It was some time after midnight that something waked me, and I sat up in the darkness and looked about and listened. I could not imagine what had roused me, but I felt that I had heard something, though there was no sound in all the night, except the low blowing of the wind and the rippling of the water against the boat.

And then, suddenly, as I sat there harking, there came over the sea from the southward the desolate mournful blowing of a foghorn. I stood up abruptly and threw all my rugs from me into the bottom of the boat.

I ran down in the direction of the foghorn, and in ten minutes or so I saw against the sky the spars of a big four-masted vessel. I dropped the sail and shipped the oars. As I pulled toward her, the sound of the horn broke out into the night in a dull roar, coming from the after-part of the vessel. I backed the boat aft, noticing as I did so that the vessel stood no more than three or four feet above the level of the sea.

Then, as I came opposite to the place where the horn seemed to be, I saw dimly that the deck rose here, and that I was come opposite to the poop. I rested on my oars. "Miss Doriswold!" I shouted. "Miss Doriswold!"

The fog-horn gave a short, impotent blare, and immediately a girl's voice called:

"Who is that? Who is that?" in a queer, frightened, breathless way.

"It's all right!" I shouted back. "We got your message! I'm the mate of the *Skylark*, the ship that got the message. I'm coming aboard."

The answer astonished me.

"Don't come on to the ship!" the voice called back to me, shrill and anxious. "Keep the boat away! Keep the boat away! There are thousands of rats —"

It broke off abruptly, and there was the sound of a pistol-shot up in the darkness. At that, I had the painter fast in a moment and, catching up my gun, vaulted aboard. In an instant the girl's voice came again:

"I'm all right. Don't come aboard, whatever you do! It's the rats! Wait for the daylight!"

Even before she spoke, I was aware of a sound along the poop like the harsh noise of several saws at work. I walked aft a few steps, groping, and knew suddenly that there was a faint, curious smell everywhere about me in the night. I paused and stared through the darkness.

"Where are you?" I shouted, and then I saw the black bulk of the chart-house vaguely through the darkness. I went forward a pace, and stumbled clumsily over a deck ring-bolt. "Where are you?" I shouted again. "I've come aboard."

"Go back! Go back! Go back!" called the girl's voice shrilly, with a note of utter fear and horror in it. "Get into the boat, *quick!* I'll explain. Go back! Go back!"

III.

There came to me in the same moment a strange sense of restlessness all about the decks, and then, suddenly, all the air seemed to be full of an odd whining noise, that rose into a horrible shrill, twittering keening of sound. I heard a massed sound, as of thousands of small scuttering bodies coming toward me at a run through the darkness. The voice of the girl came in the same instant, crying out something in a frightened voice. But I never heard what she said, for something plucked my trousers, and immediately hundreds of creatures sprang upon me and swarmed over me, biting and tearing. My gun was utterly useless, and in an instant I knew that if I would save my life I must go overboard. I made a mad, staggering run to the side of the derelict, the rats flocking about me. With my free hand I was tearing their great bodies from me and keeping them from my face. The hideous little brutes were so thick upon me that I was loaded with them. I reached the rail and got over somehow, and fell souse down into the icy cold water.

I stayed under water deliberately, as long as I could; and the rats left me and went to the surface to breathe. I swam hard until my head felt as if it would burst; then I came up, and found that I was clear of the rats. I discovered that I still had my gun in my left hand, and I was careful not to lose it. I swam forward until I was opposite the boat. I heard the girl's voice calling something to me, but the water in my ears prevented me from hearing what it was.

"Are you safe? Are you safe? Where are you?" the girl was calling.

"I'm all right, thanks!" I shouted back. "I'm in the boat. I'll wait till daylight, if you're sure you are safe."

She assured me that she was all right, now that I had come, and could easily hold out until the morning. In the meanwhile I had stripped off my wet things and got into the spares I had brought with me and for which I was very thankful now, as you can imagine. All the time, as I changed, the girl and I kept up a conversation. I asked her about food; she told me she had eaten nothing for three days and nights but had still some water, and I was not to try to reach her until daylight came to show me the position of everything.

This, however, would not satisfy me, and as I completed my dressing a sudden thought came to me. I struck a match and lit the binnacle-lamp and also the boat's lantern, which was in the midship locker. Then I hooked the ring of the lantern over the spike of the boat-hook and reached the lantern up on to the poop of the derelict, where I set it on the deck. I could see the chart-house plainly now, and a pale but very beautiful face was looking at me through the glass of one of the ports. It was Miss Doriswold, and I waved to her with the boat-hook. She opened the port about an inch and called out to know what I was going to do. I told her she would see very quickly. Then I stuck the boat-hook into the handle of the binnacle-lamp and ran to the other end of the boat, where I was able to set it inboard on the poop deck, some way farther aft than the boat-lamp.

I got the bottom boards of the boat now and set

them across from gunnel to gunnel of the boat, and then, taking my gun and a pocket full of cartridges, I stood on this temporary erection and looked aboard.

I saw a most extraordinary sight, and really a very horrible one; for in the light of the lamps the *decks were literally black and moving with rats,* and the shining of their eyes in the lights made a constant, myriad twinkling from a thousand places at once, as the rats shifted this way and that. All about the base of the house there seemed to be rats, and I could see dimly that they had been at the wood-work of the house, but as there was a steel combing in at the back of the teak, very few had been able to get in, and then only by the door, as I learned afterward.

I glanced at the port, but Miss Doriswold was not there, and as I looked there came the flare of a match and immediately the sharp report of a pistol-shot. In a minute she returned to the port and cast out a big rat, which was instantly set upon by hundreds of others in a great black scramble. Then I raised my gun so that it was just a little above the level of the poop-deck and fired both barrels into that struggling crowd of little monsters. Several rolled over and died, and over a dozen ran about wounded and squealing, but in a moment both the wounded and the dead were covered with the living rats and literally torn to pieces.

I reloaded quickly and began now to fire shot after shot among the hideous little brutes, and with every thud of the gun they lay dying and dead over the deck, and every time the living rats would leap on to the dead and wounded and destroy them, devouring them practically alive.

In ten minutes I had killed hundreds, and within the next half hour I must have destroyed a thousand, to make a rough guess. The gun was almost red-hot in my hands. The dead began now to lie about the decks; for most of the rats were destroyed and the living rats had begun to run into hiding. I waved to Miss Doriswold, and we began to talk, while the gun was cooling.

She told me she had been fighting the brutes off for the last four days, but that she had burned all her candles and had been forced to stay in the dark, only striking a match now and again (of which she had several boxes left) when the sounds at the door told her that a rat had nearly gnawed his way through. Then she would fire the Captain's revolver at the brute, block the hole up with coal, and sit quiet in the dark, waiting for the next. Sometimes the rats got through in other places, above the steel combing. In this way she had been badly bitten several times, but had always managed to kill the rats and block the holes.

Presently, when the gun was cool again, I began to shoot systematically at every rat in sight, so that soon I had killed and driven the little monsters clear off the visible parts of the poop-deck. I jumped aboard then, and walked round the house, with the boat-lantern and my gun. In this way I surprised and shot a score of rats that were hiding in the shadows, and after that there was not a rat to be seen anywhere.

"They're gone!" I shouted to Miss Doriswold, and in the same moment I heard her unlocking the chart-house door, and she came out on to the deck. She looked dreadfully haggard and seemed a little uncertain on her feet, but even thus I could see how pretty she was.

"Oh!" she said, and staggered and gripped the corner of the chart-house. She tried to say something further, but I thought she was going to fall and caught her arm to lead her back into the house.

"No!" she whispered breathlessly. "Not in there!" And I helped her to the seat on the side of the skylight. Then I ran to the boat for brandy, water and food, and presently I saw the life begin to come back into her. She told me later that she had not slept for four nights. And once she tried to thank me, but she was dumb that way —only her eyes said all the rest.

Afterward, I got her to the boat, and when I had seen her safe and comfortable, I left her there and walked the poop of the derelict until daylight. And she, now that she felt safe, slept through the whole night and far into the daylight.

When she waked I helped her aboard again and

she insisted on preparing our breakfast. There was a
fireplace in the chart-house, and coal, and I broke up
the front of one of the hen-coops for kindling-wood.
Soon we were drinking hot coffee and eating sea-
biscuit and tinned meat. Then we went out on deck
to walk up and down and talk. In this way she
learned my side of the story, and questioned me
closely on every point.

"Oh," she said at last, holding out both hands to
me, "may God bless you!" I took her hands and
looked at her with the strangest mixture of awkward-
ness and happiness. Then she slipped her hands from
me and we went again to our constant pacing.
Presently I had to send her to rest, though she would
not at first, because she felt too happy to sit still; but
afterward she was glad to be quiet.

Through four days and nights we waited for the
Skylark. The days we had entirely together; the nights
she slept in the chart-house, and I in the little
alleyway, with just a few feet below me the roll and
gurgle of the water going through the waterlogged
cabins of the half-sunk vessel. Odd whiles I would
rise and see that the lamp was burning brightly in the
rigging, so that the *Skylark* would not pass us in the
darkness.

On the morning of the fourth day, after we had
made our breakfast happily together, we went out for
our usual walk of the poop. The wind still continued
light, but there were heavy clouds to the northward,

which made me very anxious. Then, suddenly, Miss Doriswold cried out that she saw the ship, and in the same moment I saw her, too. We turned and looked at each other. Yet it was not all happiness that was in us. There was a half-questioning in the girl's eyes, and abruptly I held out my arms!

Two hours later we were safely aboard the *Skylark,* under only the main lower-topsail, and the wind coming down out of the north like thunder while to leeward the lonesome derelict was lost in huge clouds of spray.

The Haunting of the Lady Shannon

THE HAUNTING
OF THE LADY SHANNON

I.

Captain Jeller had his men aft for a few brief words as the *Lady Shannon* wallowed down-channel in the wake of the tug. He explained very clearly that when he gave an order he expected that order to be obeyed with considerable haste or there would be "consequences."

Captain Jeller's vocabulary was limited and vulgar, and his choice of words therefore unpleasing; but there was no mistaking his meaning; and the crew went forward again, shaking their heads soberly.

"Just wot I said," remarked one of them, "he's a 'oly terror!"

In this there seemed to be a moody acquiescence on the part of the others; all except one, a young fellow, who muttered an audible threat that he would stick his knife into any one who hazed him.

"That's wot you thinks," returned the first speaker. "You just 'ave a try, an' you'll find 'arf a bloomin' ounce of lead in yer bloomin' gizzard!"

"That's so," added one of the older men with conviction. "Them sort allus carries a gun in their pocket, handy-like."

But the young man looked at the other two with a sullen, somewhat contemptuous stare.

"They wouldn't dare if you chaps stuck up to them. It's just because you let them haze you. You run if they breathe on you!"

"You just wait a bit, young feller," replied the second man. "Wait till one on 'em gets his knife into yer. I've sailed with them kind, an' you 'aven't. They've ways an' means as you've no idea of. You'll learn quick enough if you runs foul of one on 'em!"

The older man finished his warning with a solemn shake of the head, to which the young fellow replied nothing; but, turning, went into the fo'cas'le, swinging his shoulders unbelievingly.

"He'll be gettin' 'arf murdered," remarked the first man.

"Aye," returned the other. "He's young an' thinks he can 'old 'is own; but Lord help 'im if he runs foul of the after-guard!"

And they also went into the fo'cas'le.

Aft, in the "glory hole," three of the 'prentices — all youngsters — sat and regarded one another with dismayed looks.

"What an old brute he must be!" exclaimed Tommy, the youngest. "If my people had guessed he was like that there would have been ructions and no mistake."

"Well, youngster," put in Martin, an older lad who had done the previous trip with the skipper, "you're in a hot shop right enough; but you'll find it a darned sight hotter if you go talking like that with the door open. They can hear every word you say up on the poop; that is, if there's not much wind."

Tommy looked startled.

Martin continued, addressing the three of them:

"See here, youngsters; what you've got to do is to fly like mad if they sing out for you to do anything, and whatever they do, never answer one of them back. Never!"

He repeated the last word with emphasis.

Tommy's eyes grew rounder.

"Why?" he said breathlessly. "What do you think they would do?"

"Do? Goodness knows! Anything, I believe. Last trip they treated one of the ordinaries so badly that the poor chap went queer — silly. Mind you, he acted like a goat and gave both the second mate and the skipper slack; but they knocked all that out of him and some of his brains as well, I believe. Anyway he went half-dotty before the end of the voyage."

"Why didn't the men interfere?" questioned the boy, warmly.

"Interfere? Not they! And if they had the old man would have shot them down like a lot of sheep."

"Didn't you tell when you got home?"

Martin shrugged his shoulders.

"Not I. The youngster cleared out — disappeared. Besides who was I to tell, and what could I have said? They'd have shut me up anyway."

"I'd never have come on the same ship again — never!"

"That depends," replied Martin. "I tried to get shoved into another but it was no use. And wouldn't I have looked pretty now if I had gone 'round telling how Toby the ordinary seaman was used by the old man and the second? Wouldn't I be in for a nice time of it, eh?"

Tommy nodded gravely; yet his eyes were reproachful.

"Still, I think you ought to have told, even — "

"Oh, stow it!" exclaimed Martin, cutting him short. "Wait until you've had the old man down on top of you; then you can begin to gas."

Tommy wisely made no reply, but began talking with the two others in a low voice; while Martin lay back in his bunk and smoked.

II.

During the next few days the *Lady Shannon* had a fine fair wind which took her well away from the land, the captain making a course sufficiently to the westward to clear the bay.

Now that they were in blue water there was no mistaking the after-guard's intentions to make things hum for the "crowd." There was no afternoon watch below, and work was kept up right through the second dog-watch, while instead of turning the men to washing down at 6 A.M. it was buckets and brooms — and holystones — as soon as the morning watch was relieved at 4 o'clock.

All this as may be imagined developed a very fair amount of grumbling among the men; but after three or four had been laid out by the first and second mates with the aid of a belaying-pin the grumbling was confined to the inside of the fo'cas'le, and the crowd bade fair to submit quietly enough to treatment far worse than would be meted out to any convict in one of our prisons.

Yet, as it happened, there was one man with sufficient pluck to make a stand for the sake of the manhood within him, and this was Jones, the young fellow who had sworn he would not be hazed.

So far he had been sufficiently fortunate to

escape the attentions of the second mate, in whose watch he was.

On the twelfth day out, however, came violent friction between them. The men were holystoning at the time, and the second, on the lookout for trouble, was "bouncing" 'round the decks and keeping them at it. Suddenly he saw Jones biting off a chew.

"Darn you, you terbaccer-eating hog!" he roared. "You just throw that plug over the side an' put some of your dirty beef on ter that stone!"

But Jones did no such thing. Instead, he slipped the plug back into his pocket. In an instant the second mate was beside him.

"I'll teach you not to do what I tell you!" he snarled, and pushed the kneeling man over on to the muddy decks with a rough thrust of his boot.

Jones fell on his right side and the plug of hard tobacco tumbled out from his pocket among the slime of water, dirt, and mud-colored sand. Immediately the second stooped for it and the next instant it was over the side.

"Get a hold of that stone!" he bellowed. "Smart now, or I'll knock the dirty face off you!"

He gave a clumsy kick with his heavy seaboot as he spoke.

The kick took Jones in a slanting graze across his right shin-bone and he gave a curse of pain. Then he scrambled on to his knees.

"Thought that'd fetch you!" said the second

mate grimly. "Get ahead with that there stonin' if you don't want any more!"

Jones made no reply and no move to go on with his work; but just stared wrathfully up at the officer.

" — — — — you!" he burst out at last.

"That's it, is it!" exclaimed the second, and ran to the starboard pin-rail from whence he took a heavy iron belaying-pin. He returned at a run.

"Now then you dirty son of a sea-horse!" he roared. "I'll show you! You open your blabby mouth to me!"

He raised the pin as he pointed to the holystone.

"Pick it up!" he shouted. "Pick it up an' get to work or I'll knock you inter next week!"

Jones picked up the great lump of holystone with an air of apparent submissiveness, but instead of beginning to work it across the gritty deck he suddenly raised it in both hands and brought it down with a squashing thud upon the second mate's right foot. The officer gave out a loud yell of agony, dropped the belaying-pin, raised his injured member, slipped and came down stern-foremost among the muck of sandy mud.

The next instant Jones had flown at him like a tiger and taking him by the throat had forced him down upon his back and commenced banging his head against the deck. The men had ceased their stoning and were looking on in mingled terror and delight.

All at once from the direction of the poop there came the sound of running footsteps; they passed along the narrow gangway which led to the little bridge, standing upon four stanchions in the middle of the after part of the main-deck.

"Ther old man!" called some one in a voice of fear; but Jones, mad with anger, was past noticing.

The following moment the skipper's face appeared over the bridge-rail, his face livid with rage. He held a revolver.

"Jeerusalem! You strike my officer! Take that! An' that! An' that!"

He was firing indiscriminately among the men upon the deck. Evidently he had been drinking, for though it was plain that he desired to perforate Jones, he only succeeded in shooting one of the other men through the calf of the leg.

Then, save for Jones and the second mate, the decks were empty of men. They had run like sheep. Up on the bridge the captain was clicking his revolver impotently. It had not been loaded in all its chambers, and he had fired off the full ones.

From further aft the first mate appeared in his shirt and trousers. He caught sight of the struggle from the break of the poop, and straight away made two jumps of the ladder on to the main-deck. Reaching the place where Jones was worrying the almost senseless officer, he took a flying kick at him, but with no effect. At that he stooped and caught him by the collar, reaching at the same time for the heavy pin which the second mate had dropped.

"Let go, you rotten fool!" he shouted, raising the pin.

"Let go, you — !" obscenely echoed the skipper from the bridge overhead.

At the same time he hurled his empty revolver at Jones. The flying weapon took the first mate on the top of the head and he went down in a heap without knowing what had struck him.

From the doorway of the 'prentices' berth there came a shrill "Hurray!" in a boy's voice. It was from Tommy, who had thus involuntarily voiced his delight at the turn which the affair had taken. The skipper caught the word and turned wrathfully. He saw Tommy and immediately threw his leg over the edge of the bridge-rail. Dropping to the main-deck, he went for the boy.

"You puppy-faced poop ornament!" he snarled. "You dare ter open your biscuit-hatch at me!"

He seized him by the back of the neck and ran him to the starboard rail. Here, grasping the end of the mizzen lower topsail brace, he shifted his grip to the youngster's arm. Then with the heavy brine-sodden rope he struck the boy furiously, beating out from him little gasping sobs. In his savage, half-drunken state he took no note of where he struck, and under one of the blows, which caught Tommy across the back of the neck, the boy went suddenly limp within his grasp.

Behind him there came a curse in the mate's voice, a dull thud and a quick choking cry from Jones, another blow, followed by a slight gurgle and then silence.

The skipper opened his hand and Tommy slid down on to the deck — quietly; then tossing down the rope-end across him he turned rapidly to see the first mate, recovered from the result of the misaimed pistol, in the act of dragging the limp body of Jones off the second mate.

Taking not the least notice of the huddled boy upon the deck, the captain walked for'ard a few steps and looked down at the insensible second. Then he roared for the steward to bring some whisky. When this was brought they forced some between the second mate's lips and when he came 'round applied the bottle to their own; after which, with the help of the steward, they got the battered officer to his room.

Returning on deck the skipper sang out for two of the men to lay aft and carry Jones for'ard. Tommy had been removed to his bunk by the 'prentices, immediately the captain and the mates left the deck and now Martin was busily engaged in bathing his head with some salt water.

III.

It was two nights later, in the first watch. The second mate had shaken off the effects of his hammering sufficiently to return to duty. To himself he had vowed that Jones — if he lived — should suffer terribly before the ship reached port. But Jones was still in a state of semiconsciousness, due to the blows that the first mate had dealt him; so that for the present the second mate had to curb his hatred and wait.

Four bells had gone and it was full night, with a bright moon shining. For a while the captain and the second mate had paced the poop, conversing on various topics, chief of which was the grinding of all insubordination out of the men. Presently in response to an order of the captain's the second mate made his way along the narrow gangway — elevated some ten feet above the main-deck —to the little bridge on its four teak uprights.

Upon the bridge was placed the "Standard" compass. In addition to the compass there were a couple of rows of wooden ornamental poop-buckets, while up through the deck of the little bridge rose a ventilator. Nothing else was kept upon the bridge; so that what followed the captain was enabled to see plainly. He saw the second mate step up to the compass and peer in at the lighted card. Then came his voice —

"Sou —"

It broke off horribly with a hoarse scream and the captain saw him throw up his arms and fall backward on to the bridge deck. Completely astounded and puzzled the skipper ran hastily along the gangway to him.

"What's up with you, Mr. Buston?" he asked, stooping over him; but the second gave back no reply.

At last the skipper reached for the binnacle-lamp. Slipping it from its place he threw the light upon the prostrate mate. It showed him the face, curiously distorted. From that his glance passed to a thin stream which trickled from beneath the man. He knelt down and turned him half over. The blood came from the back of the right shoulder.

He stood up, releasing the body, and it fell back with an inert sagging of the shoulders. He felt dazed and frightened. The thing had happened before his eyes, within twenty feet of him; yet he had seen nothing that would account for it.

The bridge stood up above the main-deck like an island and was reached only by the gangway which led from the poop. But even if this had not been so it did not seem possible that any one could have touched the second mate without the captain being aware of it. The more he turned the matter over the more he realized how inexplicable it was. Then a sudden idea came to him and he glanced upward. Had a knife or a spike been dropped from aloft. He thought not. Had that been the case then the instrument would have been visible — and there was none. Besides, the wound was behind.

Had it been caused by any one dropping a knife or spike, then it would have been in the head or top of the shoulders. There was a similar objection to supposing that a weapon had been thrown at him from the deck below. In that case the wound would have been in the front or one of the sides. It was no use; he could not solve the mystery.

He gathered his wits somewhat and bellowed to one of the 'prentices to go and call the mate. Another he sent for'ard to order every man, watch below as well as watch on deck, to lay aft. He would at least know the whereabouts of each of the crew.

The first mate came running with his gun in his hand. It was evident that he was incurably expectant of trouble. While the men were mustering the skipper told the first mate all that he knew.

As soon as the men were aft the captain made each one pass below the bridge under the light from the binnacle-lamp. Every man was thus discovered to be there, except Jones. Then the 'prentices were mustered, and all came forward except Tommy. As soon as this was done the skipper told the men to stay where they were. Then he ordered the mate to go and see if the missing man and boy were in their respective bunks. In a few minutes the first mate returned to say that they were. Then the captain dismissed the men; but without telling them of the tragedy which had occurred.

As soon as they had gone he turned to the first mate.

"See you 'ere, Mr. Jacob," he said. "Do you think as that dirty carkiss for'ard is as bad as 'e seems?"

"Yes, sir," replied the mate. "It's not him, if that's what you're thinking. He looks as if it was his turn next to slip off the hooks."

"An' ther b'y?"

The mate shook his head.

"No, sir. He's not got over that warming you gave him by a long chalk."

"If I thought — " began the skipper; but broke off short.

"Yes, sir?"

The skipper threw the light down on to the dead man.

"Wot's done it?" he asked in a voice denoting that he was at the end of his imagination. "Wot's done it?"

"Well sir, it must be one of the lousy crowd for'ard."

"One of ther crowd! Do you think as one of them'd be livin' if I'd thought as it was them!"

The first mate made no reply, and the captain continued.

"It ain't nothin' 'uman as 'as done this 'ere."

He stirred the body with the toe of his boot as he spoke. "You think, sir — "

"I don't think nothin'! I'm a long way past thinkin'. Why! I saw 'im killed with me own eyes. He was just struck dead standin' 'ere in ther moonlight. There weren't nothin' come near 'im, an' there ain't no signs of a knife, nor nothin'. I reckon as it's some one as 'e's done for, some time or another."

The mate glanced 'round the decks, silent and ghostly under the moonlight. Though he was a fairly intelligent man, it was plain that he felt a chill of unease.

The skipper went on with his uncomfortable theorizing:

"It's a dead man's ghost!" he said. "W'en that hog for'ard, as you done for, slips 'is cable, strikes me as you'll be 'aving a call — sudden!"

He touched the body with his foot, suggestively.

"I didn't know that you were superstitious, sir," said the mate.

The captain turned and looked at him steadily.

"You knowed right then," he said at length. "I ain't, but I ain't a blind fool neither! An' when I sees one of me officers knifed before me eyes, an' nothin' in sight, you can bet as I give in ter facts. I never was narrer, an' wot me eyes shows me I believes. You can take it from me right off as ther's something in this 'ere packet as ain't 'uman.''

He waved the light over the dead second mate.

"I reckon as 'e's been a bad un!" he remarked, as though to himself.

Then, as if coming suddenly to his everyday self, he gave a slight shiver which he turned off into a shrug.

" 'Ere, Mr. Jacob, let's get outer this 'ere," he said.

And he led the way, followed closely by the first mate, off the bridge. On the poop he turned to the mate.

"You take charge, mister. I'm goin' down for a snooze. I reckon you can shift 'im — " jerking his thumb toward the bridge — " as soon as it's daylight."

IV.

During the following day the captain indulged in a heavy, solitary drinking-bout; and on finding out from the steward that the skipper was hopelessly drunk the first mate took upon himself to put the second over the side. He did not fancy another night with that thing aboard.

That the first mate had taken the extraordinary event of the night to heart, was common talk in the

fo'cas'le; for he relaxed entirely his bullying attitude
to the men and in addition on three separate occasions sent word for'ard to learn how Jones was
progressing. It may be that the skipper's theorizing of
the preceding night had something to do with this
sudden display of sympathy.

With the captain being drunk, the first mate
had to take all the night-watches. This he managed
by having one of the older men up on the poop a
portion of the time to keep a lookout, while he
himself got a little rest upon the seat of the saloon
skylight. Yet it was evident to the man whom he had
called to keep him company, that the mate obtained
little sleep; for every now and again he would sit up
and listen anxiously.

Once he went so far as to call the man to him
and ask if he could not hear something stirring on the
bridge. The man listened, and thought perhaps that
he did; but he could not be sure. At that the mate
stood up excitedly and ordered him to go for'ard and
find out how Jones was. Much surprized, the man
did as he was bid, returning to say that he seemed
queer and that the men in the fo'cas'le thought he
was slipping his cable and would the first mate go
for'ard and have a look at him.

But this the mate would by no means do.
Instead he sent the man along to the fo'cas'le every
bell and between whiles he himself stood by the rail
across the break of the poop. Twice he called to the

man to come and listen, and the second time the man agreed that there certainly was a noise on the little bridge. After that the mate continued to stand where he was, glancing 'round about him frightenedly, a very picture of shattered nerves.

At half-past two in the morning the man came back from one of his visits for'ard to say that Jones had just gone. Even as he delivered himself of the news there came a distinct grating sound from the direction of the bridge. They both turned and stared; but though the moonlight was full upon everything there was nothing visible. The man and the mate faced one another — the man startled, the mate sweating with terror.

"My — !" said the man. "Did yer 'ear that, sir?"

The mate replied nothing; his lips quivered beyond his control.

Presently the dawn came.

In the morning the skipper appeared on deck. He seemed quite sober. He found the first mate haggard and nervous, standing beside the poop rail.

"I guess you'd best get below an' 'ave er sleep, Mr. Jacob," he remarked, stepping over to him. "You look as if you was spun out."

The first mate nodded in a tired manner but beyond that made no reply. The skipper looked him up and down.

"Anythin' 'appened while I was — was below?"

he asked, as though the mate's manner suggested the thought.

"Jones has gone," replied the mate harshly.

The captain nodded as though the mate's reply answered some further question.

"I s'pose you dumped 'im?" he said, nodding toward the bridge, where the second mate had lain.

The mate nodded.

"Seen — or 'eard anythin'?" beckoning again toward the bridge.

The first mate straightened himself up from the rail and looked at the skipper.

"Directly after Jones went, there was something messing about yonder." He jerked his thumb toward the bridge. "Stains heard it as well."

The captain made no immediate reply. He appeared to be digesting this piece of information.

"I sh'd keep clear of ther bridge, Mr. Jacob, if I was you," he remarked at length.

A slight flush rose in the mate's face.

"I heard from one of the boys that young Tommy seems pretty shaky this morning," he replied with apparent irrelevance.

" — — — — ther b'y!" growled the captain.

Then, glancing at the mate —

"You think — "

His gaze followed the mate's to the bridge and he did not finish.

It was noticeable after the mate had gone below that the captain for the first time made inquiries as to the state of Tommy's health. At first he sent the steward; the second time he went himself. It was a memorable fact.

V.

That night the captain and the mate kept the first watch together. At the beginning, before it was quite dark, they paced the poop and kept up an irregular conversation; but now that it was night they had drifted to the for'ard poop-rail and there leaned, scarcely speaking once in a couple of minutes.

To a close observer their attitudes might have suggested that they were listening intently. Once it seemed there came a faint sound through the darkness, from the direction of the bridge, whereat the first mate babbled out something in a strained, husky voice.

"You keep ther stopper on, Mr. Jacob," said the skipper, "else you'll be goin' barmy."

After that there was nothing further until the moon rose, which it did board away on the starboard bow. At first it gave little or no light, the horizon being somewhat cloudy. Presently its upper edge came into sight above the "Standard" binnacle, framing the bulging brass dome with a halo of misty light that gave it for the minute almost a curiously unreal spectral appearance. The light grew plainer, casting grotesque but indistinct shadows.

Suddenly the silence was broken by a strange husky inhuman gurgle from the bridge. The skipper started; but the mate never moved; only his face shone white in the glowing light. The captain could see that the little bridge was clear of all life. Abruptly as he stared there came from it a low, incredible, abominable laughter. The effect upon the mate was extraordinary. He stood up with a jerk, shaking from head to foot.

"He's come for me!" he said, his voice rising into an insane quavering shout.

From forrard and aft there came the sound of running feet. His wild cry had brought out the crew.

From the bridge there came a further sound, vague, and, to the captain, meaningless. But it had meaning to the mate.

"Coming!" he screamed in a voice as shrill as a woman's.

He sprang away from the skipper's side, and ran stumbling along the narrow gangway to the bridge.

"Come back, you fool!" roared the captain. "Come back!"

The mate took no notice, and the skipper made a rush for him. He had reached the bridge and flung his arms about the "Standard" binnacle. He appeared to be wrestling with it. The captain seized him by the arm and tried to tear him away; but it was useless. Suddenly as the skipper struggled something bright flashed over his shoulder, past his ear, and the mate went slowly limp and slid down upon the deck.

The captain wrenched around and stared. Exactly what he saw no one knew. The grouped men beneath heard him shout hoarsely. Then he came flying over the bridge-rail down among them. They broke and ran a few yards. Something else came down over the rail. Something white and slender that ran upon the captain noiselessly. The captain dodged, rushing sidewise with his head down. He butted into the steel side of the deck-house and crumpled up.

"Catch it, mates," shouted one of the men, and ran among the shadows.

The rest, inspired by his courage, closed about in a semicircle. The decks were still very dim and indistinct.

"Where is it?" came in a man's voice.

"There — there — no — "

"It's on ther spar," cut in some one. "It's — "

"Overboard!" came in a chorus, and there was a general rush for the side.

"There weren't no splash," said one of the men presently, and no one contradicted him.

Yet whether this was so or not Martin, the oldest

'prentice, insisted that the white thing had reminded him of Toby the ordinary seaman, who had been hazed to the verge of insanity by the brutality of the captain and officers on the previous voyage.

"It's the way his knees went," he explained. "We used to call him 'Knees' before he went queer."

There is little doubt but that it was Toby who, in his half-insane condition, had stowed away and worked out a terrible vengeance upon his tormentors. Though, of course, it can not be proved.

When after a sleepless excited night the crew of the *Lady Shannon* made a search of the bridge they found traces of flour upon the bridge-deck, while the mouth and throat of the ventilator in the center of the bridge was dusted with the same whiteness.

Inspired by these signs to doubt their superstitions they unshipped the after hatch and made a way to where the lower end of the ventilator opened above the water-tanks. Here they found further traces of flour and in addition discovered that the manhole-lid of the port tank was unshipped.

Searching 'round, they saw that a board was loose in the partition enclosing the tanks from the surrounding hold. This they removed and came upon more flour — the ship was loaded with this commodity — which led them finally to a sort of nest amid the cargo. Here were fragments of food, a tin hook-pot, a bag of stale bread and some ship's biscuits; all of which tended to show that some one had been stowed away there. Close at hand was an open flour barrel.

Toby had crawled at night from his hiding-place to the ventilator and, concealed there, had stabbed the officers as they came within reach.

Tommy regained his health, as did both Captain Jeller and Jacob, the mate; but as a "hard-case" skipper and a "buck-o-mate," they are no longer shining examples.